Jessica Holt is a retired teacher. She has previously published *The Man Who Changed His Name*.

Travelling with Spies is her second novel.

For my family

Jessica Holt

TRAVELLING WITH SPIES

AUSTIN MACAULEY PUBLISHERS™

LONDON • CAMBRIDGE • NEW YORK • SHARJAH

A CIP catalogue record for this title is available from the British Library.

ISBN 9781528909914 (Paperback)
ISBN 9781528909921 (Kindle e-Book)
ISBN 9781528959421 (ePub e-book)

www.austinmacauley.com

First Published (2019)
Austin Macauley Publishers Ltd
25 Canada Square
Canary Wharf
London
E14 5LQ

Part One

Recruitment

Natalie's short-lived teaching career began badly. She had started at the wrong time of year; that is the summer term when exam candidates are winding up and the rest of the school is winding down. She had been mistaken by a semi-senile deputy head as a confident and experienced English and drama teacher and, without any support, was plunged into a chaotic timetable; given the most difficult tutor group in the school; working under the most sexist and racist Year Head. The Head of English looked and spoke like an RAF Officer and the Head of Drama was a semi-professional actor; someone she only met once by accident. At the tender age of twenty-two, her career choice was a disaster. "Stick it out," advised her parents, "the pension is good."

"But I can't last till I'm sixty!"

"Don't give up. It's early days." All the advice her parents gave went spinning round her head, as she took a bus every morning feeling sick with anxiety; knowing she would have to find a way to survive the day. With zero control over her classes and no one aware of what was happening to her, she smiled at colleagues and tricked them into thinking she was in control.

She decided to resign after one term but before she did an accidental meeting took place with the tall, dark and very handsome actor, the Head of Drama, and he gave her some advice,

"Don't leave till you've made a success of teaching; then go with your self-worth intact."

"But how exactly do I do that?" Natalie's deep-set eyes widened.

"You're an actor, aren't you? Use your skill. Come down, see me teach and I'll show you the resources to help you." The resources turned out to be a large cupboard full of wigs.

Her suspicious imagination wondered whether her colleague was a transvestite. The wigs were lovingly arranged on plastic heads presumably to show their full potential.

"Wear a different one every day, play a different role every day and the kids will love it." That was Nick's advice and she never saw him again. He was the one who resigned and in her second term of teaching she became Head of Drama. She found that as her confidence grew, her teaching mesmerised her classes which always began with her arrival in a wig as a different person. The students never got tired of her entrances and the guessing games she played with them. Sometimes, they guessed immediately; sometimes, after twenty questions, they were still clueless and they knew if they hadn't discovered her identity by the end of that lesson she would return for next week's lesson wearing the same wig. She varied things a little by adding an item of costume or using a prop. Those ten minutes at the beginning of each lesson won them over for the remaining time and by the third term of teaching she was easily the most popular and inspiring teacher in the school (according to the students anyway).

But, in the land of Shakespeare, the educationalists were less enamoured of her subject; considering it to be either a waste of time or of value, only to less able or socially inept students. The only way Natalie felt any self-worth was from the students but luckily for her, this enthusiasm was passed on to their parents who were largely middle class and probably going to the theatre at least once a week unlike any of her colleagues. At one parents' evening in the summer term, a man sat down in front of her without an appointment.

"I won't waste too much of your time but I would like to offer you a job. Here is my card—please phone and make an appointment as soon as you can." Then, he said, "I am in need of your services and I don't like to be kept waiting."

Although Natalie was completely stunned and unable to speak, she took in his face and his beautiful brown eyes. He was incredibly handsome, with what she could only describe later to her friends as looking like a dark-haired Peter O'Toole or maybe more like Terence Stamp or maybe Warren Beatty. He had already gone by the time she thought of anything to say. She looked at the card but before she could read it, another person—

this time a genuine parent—sat down and smiled at her. "My son says you're a fabulous teacher and now he wants to be an actor rather than a doctor!"

For the rest of the Parents' Evening, Natalie couldn't concentrate. She found herself listening to the praise and compliments she never thought she would ever hear. But, somehow, it didn't matter anymore. She had been offered a way out, an opportunity to have a more interesting life. Instead of going to the pub, as was the normal practice after such an evening, she went home and pulled a book off her bookshelf; a guide to London. The card the man had given her turned out to be a postcard of a shop; a wig shop that looked so familiar to her. As she turned the pages of the colourful book, obviously made for tourists, she found it. It was in Covent Garden. There was a photograph in the book; the same as on the postcard and in the centre of the window of the shop on display was a long dark wig. On the back of the postcard it said 'Go and Buy'. She was overwhelmed with excitement and had it not been so late she would have gone to the pub and shared her news.

She couldn't wait until the weekend; so, she phoned in sick the next day and felt guilty about it right up to the moment she got off the tube at Covent Garden. She knew where she was headed, down to Neal Street; about half way down she found her wig shop. It was open and so delightful to walk into. On the right were shelves stacked full of wigs on beige plastic heads—ranging in colours from silver to red to purple and green; but the one she was after was in the window. On the left were shelves; this time, supporting boxes and boxes of stage makeup. At the back behind a counter, where a plump elderly woman stood wearing too much make-up, was a rail of costumes. Through her bright red lips came the words, "Can I help you?"

"Yes, I want to buy the wig in the window—the long dark one. How much is it?"

"A gentleman brought it in last week and told me I wasn't to sell it but to put it in the window." She smiled and some of the deep red lipstick had smudged her teeth.

"Well the same gentlemen gave me this and as you can see his instructions are very clear." Natalie wasn't sure what had made her say this but in a peculiar way she felt proud of her response.

"Well the same gentleman asked me to give you this." She was smiling again.

It was a receipt.

"Thank you." Natalie left the shop and went out into the narrow street into some welcome sunshine. She was puzzled. She looked carefully and besides the number on the receipt there was nothing else, no instructions. She was disappointed and wondered if her fantasies of a new direction in her life were over and perhaps a day's shopping might help her recover from the disappointment. She thought back to what the stranger had said, *Phone me to make an appointment.* She looked at the receipt again and realised the numbers were his phone number. Again, she felt proud of herself. She went to a coffee bar to think about what to do. If she phoned straightaway he would realise she had taken a day off and this would make her appear unreliable and the offer might be withdrawn. On the other hand, it would show how keen or maybe how stupid she was to go for a job without any idea of what the job was. After a strong coffee, she resolved to phone and asked to use the phone in the café. She offered to pay and the young waiter smiled and said rather conspiratorially, "Don't worry, the boss isn't around."

The phone was on the wooden counter, which was curved and cool to the touch. He answered straightaway, "Hello, it's Natalie."

"Hello, stay where you are and I should be with you in ten minutes." He put the phone down.

Natalie was so astonished she held the cream coloured phone in her hand for what seemed a very long time. Eventually, the waiter took it and placed it on the receiver. "Get through all right, did you?"

When he walked in, he came from behind the wooden bar; he must have come through a back entrance; and as before at their first meeting he was a shock to her system and because she had been facing the door she wasn't immediately aware of his presence until he sat down. He smiled at her and this time she took in the detail; his soft brown eyes, his dark wavy hair, and those movie star looks. She felt ashamed by her response to him; clearly inappropriate for a first proper meeting. He wore a white shirt with two open buttons showing dark hair on his chest. He had long dark eyelashes; small lines were everywhere; and he must have been at least forty. He was tall and slightly tanned.

"Thanks for coming. Rather sooner than I expected but I am delighted to see you." He paused and rubbed his forefinger across his upper lip.

"So, Natalie, call me Max. Would you like another coffee or something stronger?"

"Nothing, thanks. Just tell me why I'm here." She was very nervous; her voice was shaky.

He turned his head towards the waiter and ordered himself a coffee and as if he hadn't been listening he said,

"I expect you're wondering why you are here. You have quite a reputation as an exciting, inspiring teacher. I want you to resign and work for me. I require your background and skills."

"What skills?" Natalie finally found her normal voice.

"Your ability to become other people, your role-plays, your disguises, your inventiveness in a crisis – need I go on?"

Natalie was blushing but enjoying this flirtation. What else could it be?

"How did you find me, I mean why me?"

"I've already explained why, as to how I found you," he paused, "through my daughter actually. Your lessons were the only ones she could tolerate. So, I checked you out with other parents I knew; who work in a similar occupation and their children had the same opinion of you."

"So, I teach your daughter?"

"You did."

"What's her name?"

"Alex, but she's no longer there. She was expelled."

"Oh, sorry."

"Don't be, she's been difficult from the day she was born." He sipped his coffee. "I am a little concerned that you don't realise when someone is following you but we can work on that."

"You've been following me?"

"Yes, for some time."

"How long?"

"About six months."

Natalie sat back and couldn't think of anything to say but she did look at him and recognised that she was going to lose control of her life; just when she thought she had it all mapped out in front of her.

Max spoke again, "I have two questions; did you know your father was a spy and do you like sex in the afternoon?"

Natalie smiled and said, "To one question the answer is yes and to the other question the answer is no."

"Good answer. And it's up to me to work that out, is it?" Max took her hand and said, "I have to teach you two things and one of them is to like sex in the afternoon if you don't already like it because if you work for me you will be too tired at night."

"And the other?" Natalie could hardly wait for the answer.

"To make you an excellent spy." He kissed her fingers one by one.

"Like my father?" She withdrew her hand.

"Unfortunately, he wasn't that good but you will be. Do you have to return to work or shall we have lunch?"

After lunch Max began the training.

Training

Of course, Natalie was not a virgin—she was almost twenty-three and it was 1976. She had read a few books recently by feminist writers such as Germaine Greer and Kate Millet which had tended to put her off the male sex temporarily. In fact, she hadn't had sex for some time, she couldn't remember exactly. Most of the male teachers she knew spoke in misogynists' tongues; especially when sipping or rather guzzling too much beer. She had rather naively thought that younger men would be different and so, it was that she was pleasantly surprised by this older man's lovemaking that afternoon in a small but clean and comfortable hotel room in Soho. Yes, it was next to a porn shop and she was possibly, no probably, in a brothel but somehow that added excitement to that perfect afternoon. It was all about her, and her pleasure. He was a divine lover and he went on to be her mentor and handler in the mysterious world of spying. He was, of course, married after all and at least forty; any man unmarried at that age had to have something wrong with him, such was the common perception but Max was perfect and she couldn't believe her luck.

"I don't feel like returning to work tomorrow." Natalie laid her head on Max's chest.

"You must and you will finish the summer term, start your holiday, meet someone in a bar in Greece and return early for your training."

She giggled. "Is it all planned out then? And how did you know I was planning to go to Greece."

"Absolutely. And I also know who you are going with and I'm not sure I approve."

Max kissed her forehead, got up and put his clothes on.

"You do like sex in the afternoon, don't you? And you didn't know your dad was a spy?"

Natalie chose to ignore that remark and said, "And will there be other afternoons?"

"If you want." There was a slight hesitancy in his voice, which Natalie didn't like.

"How about Saturday?"

"No. Afraid weekends are for the family but you teachers finish around 3.30, don't you?"

Natalie was mildly annoyed by that comment but somehow the words just came out of her mouth, "So next Monday?"

"I can make Friday." Max smiled.

"Oh no, we teachers hit the pub on a Friday," Natalie was finding her voice with this man.

"OK, next Monday here at 4.30 and I want you to get up to speed with current events."

"So, you are giving me homework? But, I'm the teacher." Natalie stretched out her legs seductively or so she thought but, he was already completely dressed and at the door.

"And I would like you to wear the black wig."

"Anything else?"

"Yes, suspender belt and stockings, the rest I will leave up to you."

Natalie sat up sharply, furious that she had let herself be treated as a sex object.

What would Fay Weldon have to say? But, she found herself feeling too good to care.

She didn't want to shower but wanted to hold on to the afternoon fearful it may never happen again. But, she would turn up anyway.

On her way downstairs, the overweight young man with a smirk on his face said, "See you next Monday, the gentleman has booked the room, he said you liked it."

"And what else did he say?" Natalie asked aggressively.

"Nothing."

"Does he bring anyone else here?" Natalie was beginning to care enough about Max to be jealous.

"Don't know, miss, I only started today," he sniffed.

"Don't bother lying to me, I don't care."

"Then why did you ask?"

Natalie shrugged her shoulders hoping to appear nonchalant as she made a quick exit. Her mood quickly changed.

Outside, the sun was shining and the time on her watch said 5.30 pm. Surprised at how quickly the day had passed, she squinted, not so much as a result of the sun but as a result of the noise and lights of the street; the name of which she needed to take note of if she was ever to find again the building, brothel, hotel, whatever it was.

But, instead she got lost in her own thoughts and hopes for the future; in an attempt to face it head on, she would stop and force herself to look at a building or in a shop window. Her boyfriend, John, of seven years would be phoning her to arrange the evening's activities but she wouldn't be there to answer it.

The woman who lived downstairs with tight lips and a vicious tongue might climb up the stairs if she could be bothered and if she did, she would probably not leave a message for her. How did this awful woman manage to get on the teachers housing association list and get a ground floor bedsit in Muswell Hill? This woman wasn't a teacher and she was screwing a married man, the milkman no less! But, then she remembered she herself was now screwing a married man. He even wore a wedding ring whereas most Englishmen didn't. She wondered if he was telling the truth and did actually have children. It didn't make any difference; she was surprisingly without a conscience. As if by fate, she had reached the wig shop, the black wig was gone from the window. She panicked momentarily and then noticed a man in the shop. It was still open. It must have been around 6.00 pm by then but still very warm, rather untypical of English spring weather. Natalie went in. The man looked straight at her. He had the air of a man with a story to tell but was not prepared to tell it. Without a word, he handed her the wig and again, without a word, he handed her a plastic bag to put it in. She felt herself tingling with pleasure at the words Max had said, *"And I would like you to wear the black wig."* She stood in front of a large mirror stacked at the side of the shop behind numerous boxes. She put it on. It was long and straight and highlighted her green almond shaped eyes.

"It suits you," the man said.

She smiled and left and walked to Covent Garden underground. Should she have paid for it? She smiled as she bought her tube ticket.

On the train to Bounds Green, she watched how people reacted to her; the woman opposite was obese and blonde, trying hard not to notice her but Natalie felt how attracted the woman was to her and caught her eyes full of lust and then overwhelmed with embarrassment at having her thoughts read so precisely and she got off at the next stop, probably not hers. Natalie didn't normally notice gay women. She herself blushed at how she had spent the afternoon and the things she did which she had never done before. She shuddered with pleasure and her mouth felt so dry she was afraid her lips were actually stuck together. Did she smell? Did people know how she had spent that afternoon? She needed to have a bath before planning her evening, an evening she wasn't looking forward to. After seven years, she was very tired of this relationship and now she would be thinking about only one person for however long it lasted. Natalie reminded herself to buy a newspaper the next day—Oh God, it was Friday and work; and she would have to pretend that she had been ill— she would definitely cancel her evening out. She needed to go home, have a bath, watch the news, get through Friday, go to the pub. They had taken to choosing pubs that had gardens, as the spring had been remarkably warm. Someone had mentioned that there was so little rain the reservoirs might become empty! *How ridiculous,* thought Natalie and thank goodness she had booked her summer holiday in Greece. After last summer, and a fairly tricky holiday with John, this year she wanted to be free for whatever came her way but it had already come her way and she didn't want to leave London or Max; but he had told her she was to have her holiday and he would bring her back before it ended and now she needed to prepare herself for something; something that she hoped would change her ordinary small life and give her a chance to be special.

She hadn't received a message from John. Sheila, her hideous downstairs neighbour, was having sex with her milkman or at least the milkman was having sex with her. Natalie was at first horrified by the noises of hard slapping as Sheila succumbed to what sounded like very painful spanking. The flats were cheaply built and completely devoid of soundproofing. The spanking routinely lasted about twenty minutes then the milkman would loudly achieve orgasm and whether there was any pleasure for Sheila was difficult to judge, as she seemed very quiet throughout the whole proceedings. The milkman, left early evening and that enabled Natalie to have a peaceful time watching television; thinking of Max and the afternoon of the best sex she had ever experienced. She slept naked that night and allowed her mind to conjure up every detail and wondered whether Max was having the same thoughts or was he making love now to his wife. What the hell did it matter? Maybe the best option was to forget today, the job offer and get grounded back to teaching, a good worthwhile career with a great pension. She had forgotten to watch the news and decided to buy a paper on her way to work before getting on the bus. Her last thought was how hot it felt in bed and when she woke in the morning she was surprised to find herself uncovered and the duvet on the floor.

She had a quick bath and dressed in a comfortable cotton patterned skirt with a black tee shirt. She often wore black as it suited her and made her feel slim; she was five foot six and nine stone. She had a good figure and today she felt incredibly alive. She walked the half-mile walk up hill to her school. The air was warm and she thought about removing her tights but her legs were too pale. She wanted to practice wearing a suspender belt and stockings but she needed to get through Friday first and then shop on Saturday. She arrived at school having forgotten a newspaper and went straight into a first lesson without a wig. The students were surprised but found the new experience an extension of what they had come to expect or hope for something new.

"Well, this is the real wigless me, and today is all about self-awareness! I will start with a statement and let's go around the circle with a self-awareness statement."

"I am a good teacher but I don't fit in."

"I am a good dancer and I hate my brother."

"I am very clever but I am very nervous."

"I am very hungry and I need a wee."

"I am afraid of my dad."

"I want to kill my best friend."

She stopped listening at this point and a sense of panic rose up inside her at the thought of the fast approaching resignation date. Only a few weeks away and the head had promised her a pay rise and a good future if she came up with the goods. What a strange expression this was. She had absolutely no idea what the goods were. But, of course, you don't raise that with your boss who has just offered you a pay rise.

Shit, she thought, *the kids have realised I'm not listening.*

"OK, now let's see—did anyone's comments surprise you?" No response. "OK anyone's comments disappoint you? Anyone's comments make you feel uncomfortable?" Without waiting for an answer, she rose out of her chair with a flourish. "Tell you what, it's Friday let's just have a few games."

The class yelled out, "Bulldog."

This was probably the most dangerous game ever invented for children. The class would be split into two teams and each team stood at opposite sides of the hall. The objective was to cross the hall to the other side and at the same time stop the other side crossing using a very high level of violence including tripping up members of the opposing team, grabbing, pushing and so on. Whoever created this game knew what they were doing. The energy required and the anger unleashed was impressive and yet there was never a complete loss of control just the constant fear of it.

It was soon over and another Friday evening at the local pub, the closest to the school and the one most accepting of drunk teachers at closing time. For her, it meant a predictable routine of being talked down to, by teachers who taught more academic subjects; then being flirted with by all the male teachers young and old and then as they became drunk having to listen to their unsavoury lusting's after young students. She wondered whether she should have tried an evening out with John but she knew Friday night usually meant the Rugby club. That was also predictable—a game—lots of mud—a meal consisting of sausages, baked potatoes and beans and a finale of the successful and unsuccessful men singing, stripping off and then being sick. Sometimes, John would relent and change this routine and meet her for a curry; but he was usually so late, she ordered and ate before he arrived. The waiters were uncomfortable about serving a woman sitting on her own so these arrangements eventually ceased. *Must do something about this relationship,* that was her last thought as she fell asleep once her head had stopped spinning.

Waking up late to the sounds of Sheila being spanked by her milkman didn't put her in the best of moods for exploring Soho and finding her 'Hotel Brothel', as she had nicknamed it. But an early start would be good. She stomped around the flat hoping she would disrupt the milkman's rhythm but he seemed determined to complete the session, after all he did have a milk round to finish. He was in the habit of leaving the float in the middle of the road just to annoy everyone but it was a quiet road with few cars using it and it was still early. She thought she heard a squeak from the mouse like Sheila but then the milkman's roar ensured no other sound could be heard. Natalie retreated to the bathroom and had a leisurely bath, smoking her first cigarette of the day. Her headache usually cleared without any help and as she got dressed she became excited at the prospect of seeking out the place where she had experienced so much pleasure.

She walked to Bounds Green tube and got off at Piccadilly Circus and walked up Regent Street. She loved the way the street curved as if it was welcoming the tube travellers as they caught the view of it leaving the station. For Natalie, this sight evoked the times when as a student she worked for her mother at a market research firm in Swallow Street next to Veeraswamy's Indian Restaurant. She knew the market research agency had gone but Veeraswamy, the expensive and up-market Indian, would still be there. But would the Punjabi man with his splendid uniform and broad smile? All the office girls loved curry and as a special Friday lunch treat, they would all head to Berwick Street to have a curry that was as cheap as chips. One day they all fantasised that they might be able to afford Veeraswamy's.

As Natalie headed towards Carnaby Street she had the strong suspicion she was being followed, her excitement mounted as she yearned for it to be Max but she didn't want him to reveal himself too soon, she wanted him to wait. She decided to wander slowly round Carnaby Street trying hard to appreciate why it was so popular and fashionable in the sixties. She was a little too young to grasp its significance to the culture of London then and now it seemed to lack any sense of itself at all. It was full of shabby shops and tourists; a little early it was still only the beginning of May. Why was it so hot? It wasn't this hot in England at any time in the summer. She hadn't really dressed for heat having on a jumper and trousers and even socks. Time to buy some suitable clothes for the day but not here. She would head for Oxford Street, buy something summery and, of course, the suspender belt and stockings. She would then feel more comfortable for her tour of Soho.

Her favourite shop at the time was Jane Norman and it didn't disappoint. She bought a cotton knee length dress with slight shoulder pads and a pretty floral design. The pale brown background was a great contrast to the pinkish flowers. She kept it on, put the winter clothes in the plastic bag and strode out with the sun on her bare legs. She felt good. Where to buy suspenders and stockings? Soho, of course, and as she walked up to turn off Oxford Street towards Soho Square on the corner she found a small shop that sold all sorts of strange clothing and what she assumed were sex toys. Inside, she was proud of herself, as she showed no signs of embarrassment as she wondered around looking at the briefest of briefs some of which were crotch-less. There was every kind of dildo with lumps, without lumps, all sizes, all colours and some weird shapes. She eventually found what she was looking for.

"Would you like to try it on?"

"Why?" Natalie was surprised at the sharpness in her voice but then realised she wanted to get out of the shop as quickly as she could. She felt out of place and slightly ridiculous and sweat was pouring down her face. The temperature had to be in the seventies outside and even hotter in the shop. She paid and left to seek out a newspaper and a sit-down in Soho Square. In Soho Square, she found herself surrounded by people sitting on the grass, as all the benches were full. It seemed everyone needed a break from Oxford Street. The Square was always popular in the summer, and rightly so, with its pathways leading to a small mock Tudor pavilion as its centre piece but with nowhere to sit she turned up Dean Street and headed down Meard Street, down Wardour Street and into Wilkes Court which contained nothing but sex shops, striptease joints and tattoo parlours. It seemed to cram in everything that Soho stood for and could offer and more. She felt claustrophobic, as the crowded passageway was jammed with men looking for sex or maybe just looking as she was. Around the corner, on Brewer Street, was Lina Stores. This was, she believed, the best place to buy Italian delicacies ranging from coffee to salami, stocking genuine Italian oils and wines. Natalie went in as if to find a sense of what was normal and was overwhelmed by the variety on the shelves. The different shaped pastas, fresh and colourful. She lingered but had no idea how to respond to the small round Italian lady who asked, "Can I help you?"

She left the shop and tried to stay on the mission, seek and find Hotel Brothel!

Crossing over, she was startled by Raymond's Revue Bar—it seemed to dominate the streets in all directions and that was without the neon lights that would come on later that evening. This was the place you could see full frontal nudity with respectable people—I don't suppose it was a family show but presumably it was more tasteful than what was on offer in the remainder of the neighbourhood.

By contrast, a minute's walk on down Wardour Street was Soho Church. Natalie smiled but walked quickly on down to Old Compton Street. Her childhood had been spent in church every Sunday and that was enough for one lifetime. The street was full of pubs including Compton's and Admiral Duncan but what attracted her was Bottle Gerry's. Behind glass cabinets were bottles of gins, whiskies, brandies many of which were £50 and over. Natalie didn't drink spirits but the collection of different shaped glass and pretty colours were striking—you wanted to look and read the labels. The day was passing and Hotel Brothel continued to elude her, as did current events. She had no desire to buy or read a newspaper. Perhaps, this would be her rebellion. She knew as much as she needed to know anyway. Harold Wilson was gone. Rhodesia was kicking off. Peron was deposed. Callaghan was Prime Minister. Jeremy Thorpe was in trouble. There was an earthquake in Italy. There was an on-going Cod war with Iceland. In fact, she was rather proud of her current affairs knowledge.

She was hot and tired so decided to sit and have a drink in the nearest café and try to figure out where she had spent last Thursday afternoon.

The fan was whirring in the small dark café with only four possibly six small round wooden tables. Along the window side, was a breakfast bar made of solid dark wood; rather oppressive, but the light from the window was appealing and as she sat down on a high wooden stall a man sat next to her. He smiled at her and said without any embarrassment, "You have good legs."

Natalie thought about slapping him but in her experience physical responses never ended well. She recollected with some regret being at her own party, a farewell to her friends as they headed off to university. Her jealous sister had tried to terminate it at 11.00 pm. Having refused her sister's request hysteria set in and Natalie had resorted to what she believed was a tried and tested cure for such a condition but the slap led to an increase on the histrionics scale from 5 to 10 with her sister rolling on the floor exposing her white unflattering knickers. The only thing lacking was a frothing mouth. She blotted it from her memory and looked at the man straight in the eye. He spoke again, "Do you know who runs Soho?"

For a moment she had no idea what he meant and before she could suggest anything he answered, "The Maltese."

Again, before she could answer he said, "I have ordered you a coffee; milk, no sugar." He smiled.

It wasn't an unpleasant smile and for an older man in his fifties, she guessed, he was wearing well. "Thank you."

The coffee arrived remarkably quickly and he spoke again, "I have a proposition. I find you very attractive and I know other men will do too. You will be treated well and paid a great deal of money."

Natalie smiled and thought to herself, *What is it about me lately with everyone offering me a job.*

"I see you like the idea."

Natalie wondered if she should play along while she drank the coffee. Surely this wasn't the same as accepting a drink or agreeing to dance with a man. The rule was clear. You didn't, unless you wanted to stay the whole evening with the buyer.

"The idea of what?"

"Of earning a minimum of £1000 a week under my protection working in the best hotels with the richest clients."

"And what about the holidays? I am a teacher."

At this the man laughed, "Of course, I will personally take you wherever you want to go."

"That's very kind but I will have to decline as I have already been offered a new job with exciting prospects."

He stopped smiling and said coldly, "If you change your mind you can leave me a message at this address. I hope you will change your mind."

He left. Natalie gulped her coffee down and asked the waitress for a glass of water. She was suddenly a little frightened but at the same time flattered and fantasised about being a top-class call girl. She went to the toilet and looked in the mirror. She thought again as she often did of the time she asked her mother if she was attractive. "You're all right" came the less-than-enthusiastic answer.

Leaving the café, assuming she didn't have to pay she found herself without realising it that she was on her way to the address the Maltese man had given her. Leaving Soho, she felt a strange compulsion to find the address and walked down Regent Street and passed the same shops she had earlier that day. She turned into Swallow Street and looked at the huge wooden door with the number nine prominent in brass. She looked up at the floors with their large windows and lace curtains – rather tasteful she thought for a brothel. But as the Maltese man had said only rich clients for her.

As she looked up at the windows, a woman's face looked at her from the first floor. She smiled at Natalie who looked back taking in the beauty of her face, heavily made up like Dusty Springfield with dark false eye lashes, thick eye shadow almost obscuring the eyes. She wasn't young but before Natalie could even smile back someone tapped her on the shoulder, the woman retreated and she released the lace curtain taking away from Natalie any chance of further observations. She shuddered and turned quickly towards Max. He was smiling down at her and whispered seductively in her ear, "I've been following you all day."

"I knew it."

"No, you didn't or at least if you did you put it out of your mind. This isn't the place we spent the afternoon."

"I know but in case you haven't realised yet, I have very little sense of direction. But, I am proud of myself because I found this place without much difficulty."

"You want nothing to do with this place or the man who gave you his card. You couldn't find it could you? Our place?"

He had taken her hand and started to play with her fingers

"I was very confused when I left and Soho is just a muddle of sex shops, it's particularly busy today and it's so bloody hot."

"That's enough excuses, you failed your first test." He then touched her hair lightly and said with what she thought might be some tenderness. "I couldn't wait till Monday."

Natalie said nothing.

"Let's go to The American Bar for a cocktail." They held hands as they walked to The Savoy she treated herself to a gin-based cocktail with Martini mixed with fresh lemon and lime juice all in perfect balance.

"So, when exactly did you know you were being followed?" Max was drinking a Mojito.

"As soon as I got to Carnaby Street or maybe a little before."

He leant forward and said in a smug tone, "I started following you from your flat in Muswell Hill."

Natalie giggled, "Did you see the milk float?"

"Yes, and I heard the milkman." Max smiled. "How often do you have to put up with that?"

"Mainly the weekends and sometimes he manages a week day evening."

"Do you complain? Or is there some reciprocal arrangement?"

Natalie ignored his probing, "Can we eat? I'm starving and I don't normally drink spirits."

"I was hoping you'd be hungry, they have a great fish restaurant here."

"No, I'd like room service," she felt bold.

"OK, here's the key, go upstairs and put the suspender belt and stockings on."

Before Natalie could express her surprise, he said with a smile, "I followed you all round that shop."

"I haven't got the wig with me."

"Just lie on the bed and let me do the rest."

The food had gone cold by the time they had finished and the wine was warm but they drank it anyway. She knew he would be leaving soon and that made her feel incredibly sad but he gave her a number to call and told her they could meet anytime she wanted.

As he left, he handed her a file.

"When you have read this, absorb it and be ready to be tested on it and call me."

"I like this room better than the other one," she spoke slowly.

"So do I, but it will be somewhere different next time. The room is for the night, so sleep well and remember next time bring the wig." The door shut.

Natalie finished the warm wine but couldn't face the cold food. She stretched out in the double bed and recalled as much as she could of the lovemaking. She fell asleep around eleven having looked in the file but was too tired to read it. She woke early and reached for the file stored under the bed. She noticed a map of Berlin, a photograph of an elderly man in his fifties, silver hair and a moustache. When she saw her own photograph with the black wig on she realised this would indeed be her first mission. The details that followed included a drama teacher going on secondment to research Bertholt Brecht in his role as director of The Berliner Ensemble, which was his theatre after the war. He had returned to settle in the Socialist society of his dreams having been in exile during the rise of Nazism. This was Max's plan—a year in Berlin.

She knew of teachers who took a year to develop their careers or work on particular projects. Maggie, the schools Head of Music, was a good example building up the music in schools on the island of Barbados. That sounded a good way to spend a year. Another teacher had done an exchange going to Australia and the Australian teacher coming to England. But, this had no appeal for Natalie. She didn't speak a word of German and East Berlin was obviously a miserable place. There was another picture, a young and very good-looking man, the German speaker who was to accompany her as her husband—*Oh shit what have I got myself into? I need to get back, have my pill, do my week's planning.* Sunday became a complete blur and she paced the small bedsit trying to find a way of not taking the job but keeping Max. She couldn't find the courage to phone anyone and wallowed in indecision sitting on her double bed, with the fridge empty, nothing to watch on the small black and white TV. Her grey plastic covered armchairs depressed her, given to her by a teacher she didn't like but insisted on being her friend. The small wooden table that her dad had helped her to varnish was too dark and the surface was lumpy – how could you go so wrong varnishing a table?

The phone rang in the hall; it was on the wall right outside her door. She hoped it was Max but when she heard John's voice she wanted to scream.

"Where have you been all weekend? We have all been worried. I went to your mum and dad's and they hadn't seen you."

Natalie interrupted him and stated as calmly as she could,

"I have been catching up on my marking."

"What? You're a drama teacher not an English teacher."

"Well I did a cover on Friday and the class were very keen so I marked their work, they wrote plays." John sighed; he had no interest in her work. For a young man with a chemistry degree he had been a disappointment to her, refusing to get a job, living with his parents and taking the dole money every week. Funnily enough the unemployment office itself finally offered him a job that he accepted "Only short term," he assured everyone but he was still there.

"I'm not coming out tonight John," and as she said this she wondered if she had the courage to dump him over the phone but that was actually cowardice not courage, she would do it face to face when she next saw him.

As she put the phone down, she resolved to decide for herself about her future, it all seem so tied up with men. I must decide for myself. She needed a friend to guide her through this momentous evening and it turned out to be half a bottle of gin accompanied by slim line tonic that clarified her thoughts and feelings. She would get the chairs covered with smooth plum-coloured soft material, she would buy by a cheap pine table from Camden Town market and she would go to Berlin.

More Training

On her rapid return from Greece, with her companion Hans, Natalie hadn't gained any further knowledge about the mission. Hans spoke very little, though he did tell her he was from Frieberg, an attractive large town close to the Black Forest or what was left of it.

Natalie smiled and joked, "Same with Sherwood Forest, last time I went I couldn't find it. No wonder Robin Hood was hard to capture!" He didn't appreciate the joke and she realised it didn't make much sense either. Their first meeting gave her something to think about on the plane. She was nervous about flying, about meeting Max again and about the future. The thoughts of her last night in Greece amused her and soothed her in equal measure.

On arriving at the club, which was a short walk down a stony pathway towards the sea, Natalie and her friend Diana were surprised to see Jenny and Miriam there with the boys they had picked up at the taverna and somehow this made Diana angry and predictably she then set out to prove she was the most desirable of all. Natalie had two options, go home and get a good night's sleep or watch as the ladies fight it out in the smoke-filled, blue and grey lit club on the beach. She decided to stay and watch the scene play out but needed to drink a good deal more to encourage the amusement juices to flow. She moved through the dancers not recognising the song and sat at the bar awaiting service.

She smiled at the bar man but as always, she felt invisible on occasions like this. Her mother's comment would return at times like this, "You're all right." That had set back her confidence for some time and she knew that if she ever had children her answer would be very different. She had grown her hair over the winter and that had been a chore as it was extremely thick, wavy and hard to manage taking up to three hours to dry but she hadn't regretted it as it was beautifully highlighted to a deep blonde and men now found her very attractive when they took the trouble to look. Always believing her nose a little on the large size and her eyes too small and deep set, she hadn't got Di's confidence regarding eye contact. This was the key to everything and she was prepared to use it this evening. After all, her holiday companions were somewhere doing everything to establish their female superiority so why shouldn't she? She finally got the attention of the bar man and ordered an entire bottle of Retsina. She took a cigarette from her bag and before she could light it herself a man stretched round her and lit it for her. He stood very close to her

As she turned, he smiled at her and said, "Hello."

"I can light my own cigarettes, you know."

"I know but I would like to practice my English."

She fantasised about being bold and sexy and talking in clichés like "Let's not waste time here or come back to my villa." Or just kissing him would be nice as he had very beautiful round blue eyes and a full mouth. He spoke again, "You have beautiful hair." He smiled at her.

"I know." She noticed how blond and straight his hair was, long the way she liked it.

"You must be Hans."

On arriving at Gatwick, she had expected to land and be greeted by rain as was the usual story but instead it was hotter than Greece! Max was there and she knew she wasn't allowed to show any affection in front of others so she just stared at him. He shook hands with her companion and smiled at her. He looked brown, had he had a holiday with his family? She knew he wouldn't answer the question so she kept it to herself. Hans spoke first,

"It's hot here for England." It suddenly occurred to Natalie that he had no German accent. As a drama teacher she was not good with accents or so she had been told and this proved the point to her.

Max replied, "It's been like this since the beginning of May. There's a drought on and no need to holiday abroad."

"Did you?" She was quick to ask hoping there might be some clue in his answer.

"The car is across the road." Max chose to ignore the question.

Max was driving with Hans in the front. She hoped they would be travelling straight to a hotel, desperate to be alone with him but they were not driving towards London.

"Where are we going?" she asked.

"To the training camp." Still there was no sign of their previous intimacy. But their eyes met in the rear-view mirror and she saw in his glance what she hoped to see.

After all he couldn't have put the last night they spent together behind. But then it was well documented that men viewed sex differently. For them it had little to do with love.

The journey to the camp in the Brecon Beacons took eight hours. They stopped at a Little Chef for a meal that was hard to stomach after the fresh salads and barbecued meats Natalie had feasted on every evening in the Greek taverna. Here she was back in the land of over-cooked vegetables, tasteless meat and too little alcohol at meal times.

God, she thought, *when is this country going to catch up!*

Back in the car she reflected on her last term at school. It had been good so good she almost changed her mind about the so-called secondment and when she expressed this to Max he paid more attention to her than ever.

In the summer term she had decided to have her hair permed and lightened. The experience had not worked in quite the way she had anticipated. She was waiting for Max to finish work and he was delayed so, on an impulse, she went to a hairdressers in Old Compton Street, which amusingly didn't have a name. Thinking a perm and highlights would not be a problem, though a clue might have been the fact she was the only customer. She was rather surprised by the fact they still used a thick plastic cap with holes through which the hair was painfully pulled. She had been used to foils delicately wound round carefully chosen strands. It was too late to change her mind but after 20 minutes alone in the shop her head suddenly felt on fire. Her shrieks brought the lone hairdresser from the back of the shop by which time Natalie had ripped the hideous cap from her head and was shrieking. The middle-aged man, who probably wasn't a qualified hairdresser, guided her roughly to the sink where some relief came from the cool water. The next shock was to see she had gone completely blonde and curly, how that was achieved remained a mystery.

The hairdresser offered to start again but Natalie wasn't prepared to spend any more time in the shabby over-heated place and became uncharacteristically brave,

"I can't trust you to put this right and I'm not paying."

And without looking back she flounced out of the shop and into the blazing heat.

Her first thought was that Max wouldn't recognise her and that caused her more stress than the idea that her own mother might not recognise her. She decided the solution was to return to the wig shop she had been to many times before and buy a wig, not a black wig but something she liked herself and something she felt would reflect her own personality.

As she arrived at the shop Max was already there and Natalie shuddered at the thought of his displeasure. He smiled and simply said, "Had your hair done I see."

"Do you like it?"

"All men like blondes and I think it suits you, for now."

Max's words proved to be very accurate as on her return to work in that final summer term the men paid her much more attention than she had ever known. The pattern was the same

"I like what you've done to your hair." A slight smile from one of the male teachers she didn't particularly like.

Later that day a different male teacher, one she did quite like said, "Are you up for a drink this evening after work?"

After a few drinks:

"Can I take you home?"

"No." Natalie smiled. "It's a beautiful evening and I want to appreciate it on my own, but thanks." She always tried to be polite.

Natalie had befriended a biology teacher, he was not particularly popular with the staff and she felt rather sorry for him. He was tall and broad with a strong Devon accent. He was terribly unattractive with a particularly shiny pinkie and sweaty complexion and a red bulbous nose but she felt safe with him, she knew he was in love with her and she knew he would never try anything and that made it perfect. He would do anything for her and that was an unusual experience as most men she knew wanted something back but not Simon he was contented just to be with her. So, the invitation came to go on the annual biology field trip to Wales, a place known as Devil's Bridge. She had yearned to leave London in the heat and saw this as a holiday rather than any form of work. She accepted and looked forward to a week away.

It was a good time to finally break with John, she hadn't seen him for two weeks, avoiding his phone calls and not responding to any messages left for her at school.

She got home on Friday evening, all set to shower and change for the usual Friday at the pub but she couldn't leave this decision any longer so she phoned him up and they agreed to meet for a drink in Hampstead. The Flask was set in one of the prettiest narrow alleys in Hampstead village. The hanging baskets outside the pub were thriving despite the lack of rain. She reflected how boring it must be to have to water these flowers at least twice a day. Most people were outside trying to keep cool on this May evening. As she turned down the alley, her heart sank as she saw John surrounded by his university friends all of whom had come to London.

Natalie's permanent state of positivity rose to the occasion and after all they were a very entertaining bunch of young men. There was Howard with long blond hair though not as blond as her own! He was from Manchester and extremely funny with a dry, intelligent humour refusing to be brought down by any personal crisis such as no job and nowhere to live. He was short for a man about five foot two inches but Michael from Liverpool was even shorter possibly not even five foot and with long dark hair. They made a comical couple. His accent made everything he said funny; he too was jobless and homeless. But then Jack, the tallest and handsomest of them all offered to let them stay with him in his girlfriend's flat. She seemed acquiescent enough and agreed despite the flat being one-bedroomed. She said they could stay as long as they went out three times a week so her and Jack might have sex. Everyone thought this was a reasonable enough request. Natalie thought the girlfriend was mad to have her flat crowded out by unemployed young men. She was the only one with a job but it dawned on Natalie when she finally met Sharon, Jack's girlfriend that she screamed insecurity. She was thirty, working class, uneducated and totally besotted with Jack and who could blame her. Jack was far more suited to Meryl who though a little on the short side was very intelligent and very attractive. They were both there Meryl and Sharon and the close-knit group of friends and though Natalie didn't mind female company she actually felt more relaxed with just the boys. She needn't have worried because when they saw her with her new hair colour, they surrounded her with their bodies and their compliments. She told the story of the hair with a good sense of pace and more than sufficient wit. They responded with their own stories based around barbershops and what past girlfriends had experienced under the scissors. Everything sounded so much funnier in their northern accents.

It was a pity she would probably never see these entertaining and warm individuals again. As she sat down in the Indian restaurant, sadly today no longer there, she wondered what they saw in John. It was the Friday night ritual for them. Get drunk at The Flask, walk up the hill towards the tube, cross over and order Madras. She always had a Chicken Pathia as it was slightly less hot but still spicy enough to ruin Saturday morning with her bloated stomach only returning to normal by Saturday evening.

She had been dosing in the back of the car and woke up to see Max smiling at her through the mirror.

"We're going to stop and get some petrol and something to drink."

"Good," she replied, "I need the toilet."

Hans said nothing and Natalie wondered what they had been talking about. She negotiated a rather smelly, unhygienic toilet with some expertise gained in Greece. She had no objections to the Grecian hole in the ground style as long as it was clean and sometimes, even in Greece, they were. She looked forward to the day when petrol station toilets were clean enough to sit on the seats but until they were run by women, that was only a pipe dream. On coming out she bumped straight into Max and she grabbed her moment with him. She was proud of the passion she demonstrated and fully satisfied with his response. When they had stopped kissing he simply said, "I like your hair."

"Funny that most men do." She hoped he was jealous. The perm had almost grown out but the blond had stayed as a result of so much sun both in Greece and at home.

Back in the car she drew her mind back to the ending of what had been a largely unhappy relationship for her. It wasn't just the poor sex but it was the lack of aspiration and the end of the relationship summed that up. The Friday evening had been jovial and hugely enjoyable. She looked at them, his wonderful group of friends and kissed them all goodbye with great affection and John, probably driven by jealousy offered to take her home. This was the god given opportunity she had been looking for. She left him at Turnpike Lane Bus station – a gloomy place even on a warm night. A circular bus station poorly lit with the wooden benches damaged not only by offensive graffiti but also by slats missing and nails dangerously poised but he simply lay on the one by the tube exit and cried. She had to tell him many times it was over. He seemed shocked and bewildered and that fed her resolve. She hadn't meant to do it in such a heartless and hurtful way and when he still refused to accept her words, she simply walked away and didn't even look back.

She found the only way to cope with this journey to Wales was to sleep or rather just to dose, as the roads were too bumpy for sleep. The air was still, no inkling of moisture, all the windows of the Ford Anglia were open but that made no difference to the temperature. It had to be 80 degrees and it was seven in the evening. Again, she thought about John and wondered why she had wasted so many years, lacking the courage to say goodbye. She had tried to start new relationships but the men she chose always had commitments elsewhere and one young man had a girlfriend who had another lover and yet he still rejected her advances. She was baffled more than hurt. At college she took someone she fancied to bed and sex lasted all of 30 seconds! She closed her eyes.

"We'd better stop somewhere soon as I'm getting a little tired."

"I can drive," Hans spoke for the first time in four hours.

"No, you're as tired as me and here is where we'll stay."

A small hotel appeared at a curve in the small road a pub called The Swan, painted white of course with small windows on each of the two floors. The smell of musty carpets greeted them alongside a rotund ugly man with a strong Welsh accent behind a dark wooden reception desk. He rang a bell and a young boy appeared and carried the luggage up to three separate rooms. Natalie continued to fight for Max's attention but he hastened to his room, which was on the second floor next to Hans. She was parked on the ground floor and she was so furious she simply washed her hands and face and went straight to the bar and ordered a large gin and tonic. The small Welsh lady who served her must be the wife. She smiled revealing brown stained teeth.

"Do you have any ice?"

"I'll see if we have any in the freezer."

"And where's the cigarette machine?" Natalie was rattled

"In the corridor by reception, I'll get you some ice."

"And lemon please."

Natalie had trouble with the machine but that was fairly normal, nothing a good slam wouldn't solve. The wallpaper was truly grotesque beige with maroon birds. At least the carpet was plain, green, her least favourite colour. She sat alone until Hans joined her.

"I thought you'd be here."

"Well you are right but I'm not staying unless we have a proper conversation."

"What do you want to know?"

"Are you a spy, I mean have you done this before?"

"Yes, I was recruited at university."

"Which one?"

"Berlin."

"By whom?"

"Max."

The Welsh woman interrupted, "Any more drinks? Only I close the bar at 9.00."

"Yes, I'll have a bottle of gin and a bottle of tonic and more ice and lemon, thanks. And put it on the other gentleman's bill."

"You seem very agitated," Hans remarked and looked away.

"I am."

"Because of Max?"

"I don't really have any expectations, I mean he's married and like you I am just one of his recruits."

"I think you are probably more than that. Let's get something to eat if we are going to drink the night away. I expect the restaurant will also shut soon."

They turned left out of the bar past reception and into the small dining area that had no more than three tables with Max sitting at one of them. Natalie toyed with the idea of sitting at another table but decided that would be childish.

"You haven't changed then?" Max's question was directed at her but she still had on her favourite lilac and blue short halter neck dress that showed her tan and her bare and well-shaped shoulders. She knew the effect she was having on both men.

"I washed my hands and put on some lipstick but if you don't think I'm presentable enough for such a stylish hotel I'll sit over there on my own with my bottle of gin."

"Don't be so sharp with me it's making Hans feel uncomfortable."

Natalie suddenly felt her attempt at being harsh was wasted, he knew exactly how to rule her emotions and manipulate her behaviour, and the fact that she became impatient with it at times didn't help.

Instead she said no more and just listened. She ate the food, which turned out to be quite good, at least it was fresh, roast lamb and vegetables followed by apple crumble and custard, served by the young boy who took their suitcases. When she had finished she got up and said, "I'm going to have a bath and straight to bed. Travelling always makes me tired."

"Good idea," Max smiled at her and she left the table taking the gin with her.

Later, when he slipped into bed beside her he whispered in her ear,

"I want you to do two things for me tonight, give up drinking alcohol and stop smoking."

"Is that all?" The gin made her laugh when she wanted to be severe with him.

The next morning Natalie was last to the breakfast room, hungry and happy. She sat next to Hans and opposite Max. The tan suited his dark hair and brown eyes. He had on an open neck white shirt showing the right amount of chest to arouse her desire and other women's curiosity. He always wore dark, smart trousers, often navy blue. Today he looked more like Warren Beatty than Terence Stamp.

"Good morning," he said quietly, "I've ordered you full English as it's very good here."

"You're the boss," she replied.

"Did you sleep well?" asked Hans.

"We both did," Max, answered for her.

"So, what's the plan Max?" asked Natalie rather dreading the answer.

"Well, we move on to our training camp and you train, it's a couple of hours from here."

"Will you be staying with us?" Natalie was hoping he'd say yes but wasn't surprised when he said no.

"I will leave you at the gates and return as soon as you have acquired all the skills you need to complete the mission. I hope that doesn't take us beyond Christmas and then off you go in the New Year." He looked around the small breakfast room already knowing it was empty.

"You will begin with the physical aspects of training including firearms followed by training in interrogation techniques, analysis, decision making and action planning."

"Here you are!" A cheerful Welsh voice took them by surprise.

"Full breakfast for everyone, all the sauces on God's earth, salt, pepper, orange juice, jam, marmalade, toasts. I'm the daughter by the way on holiday from university. I'm hoping to become a doctor; I'm clever enough but not hard working enough."

She looked at Hans as if you could eat him for breakfast. She lingered and actually thrust her lower body towards him, Natalie giggled but the men seemed to be uncomfortable.

"Going training, are we? Take me with you Max." The young woman now moved towards him.

"Not today, Rosie," Max answered with a smile that suggested some intimacy between them. Natalie was seriously jealous and nearly hit the girl. But Max, with a small tilt of his head, indicated this would not be acceptable. Natalie was reminded of her friend Diana, always dependent on the attention of men and Diana was good at getting male attention as Natalie found to her cost many times in London. Arranging an excursion with Diana usually meant Diana had a variety of admirers throughout the evening which meant Natalie would often have to tolerate the less attractive male until a plan was hatched for some kind of a polite disappearing act; but experience had taught Natalie to stick with the first set of male predators, at least that way only one exit strategy was required. Diana would still be there in Greece on holiday.

The drive from the small hotel was short and beautiful passing through small villages round seriously small winding roads where a vehicle coming the other way might cause serious hold-ups. Natalie had recently been to Wales with the school but didn't recognise the landscape. It was very brown and suffering from the now permanent heat wave. She recalled how the school trip to Devil's Bridge might have been cut short, as the daily tankers of water had stopped coming. But the Head of Biology was determined that his field trip would carry out the ten days booked and found a rather superior alternative accommodation, that of Aberystwyth University. Natalie had been sharing her hut with a rather mature self-assured female teacher from the other school who on waking said the same thing every day

"Time for the three F's!" Natalie knew she would have to ask sooner or later what she was referring to but waited to the third day and was told with great enthusiasm, "Face, feet and fanny."

Natalie couldn't think of a reply and hoped that was the end of their communication for the day. Despite being lonely Natalie had not been drawn to this older woman, an unnatural blonde with an intense desire to make her feel inadequate in some way. Natalie already knew she was the token female teacher who knew nothing about biology and resented this woman's need to remind her by boring her to death with Latin names for flowers, bushes and even insects.

Turning into a small dirt track Max slowed the car down and she saw wire fences on both sides at least ten foot high leading to a barrier with two soldiers standing on each side. This appeared to be the training camp. Max showed them some forms, which one of the soldiers took a cursory look at and the barrier opened slowly.

Max looked at her and smiled. "OK, I'll drop you here and pick you up when it's done."

"What?" Natalie shouted out with horror.

Hans was already out of the vehicle and walking up the path, his idea of being tactful, she supposed.

"Yes, you're on your own for now but I will keep in contact I promise." Max said this so sweetly she almost cried and when he repeated the words I promise in a tone that indicated he meant it she was happy to get out of the car. The barrier closed behind her.

Max

As Max reversed up the dirt track road he convinced himself that this was the best way. To leave her at the barrier had been as painful for him as he knew it was for her. He couldn't reveal to her how much he had missed her and how he had loved watching her come through the airport exit. It was too soon and too risky. Her skin was a light brown, not too brown after all he hadn't let her stay long enough in Greece for that. He had selfishly brought her back sooner than was necessary as once his holiday was over he wanted hers to be. Her hair seemed even blonder than when she left and he liked it that way. The dark wig was sexy and made him feel less unfaithful to his wife but the relationship had now gone beyond all that. He would have stayed at the training camp given half the chance but he was called back to London.

Max had had an unusual childhood. He had been born to a well-educated father who had become an engineer supervising the building of bridges all over the world. On the occasion of Max's birth, his father Ronald was working in Cuba. Max's mother may have been well-educated too but you would never have realised. Rebecca, his mother, was known only for her looks and photos of her could only reveal some of her real beauty. She was tall with long flowing light brown hair. Having given birth to Max in St Mary's hospital in Paddington in 1932 she left after only two days, rather unusual at the time and considered very rash by the matron of the ward she was told in no uncertain terms, "Be it on your own head."

Rebecca didn't bother to reply and took Max home to their London flat, breast fed him on demand, again unheard of at the time and a rather unusual occupation for a middle-class lady anyway. Bottle was best but Rebecca was always unconventional and in any case, she simply thought it was a matter of common sense, no getting up and moving from one cold room to another, no bottles to sterilise just put him on the breast and carry on with what you happen to be doing. When she had regained her figure, she put Max in a pram and took him to the local travel agent where she booked them on the next flight to Havana – one way.

Ronald was not surprised to see her as she had always accompanied him wherever he went however dangerous or unappealing. He didn't approve of having his young child transported at such a young age to what he considered a rather uncivilised place but she was the perfect hostess and as such very persuasive and helpful in his line of work. She never lifted a finger in the house, kitchen or garden enjoying telling servants what to do and how to do it. He loved her not just for her beauty but for her acute observations of the many people she met around a dinner table. She kept a close eye on current events simply to be able to express an unconventional view over a cocktail. Max's early childhood consisted of chasing butterflies, avoiding rather large spiders and making honey with his nanny. He believed this would go on forever but abruptly they returned to England when he was seven.

The war with Germany had started and Max wondered why his parents chose this time to return to their flat in London. It was already turning from autumn to winter and both he and his mother yearned for the Cuban sun. Memories of days paddling in the warm Caribbean water, watching the fisherman bringing in their catches and eating tender pork with the skin crisped up so that you almost broke your teeth as you ate it but the taste was divine and worth the effort. The colourful fruit and the misshapen vegetables seemed like a dream to Max as he now experienced the misery of one cold after another. In bed with a hot water bottle and yet another cold Max remembered how he overheard his parents' rowing. The long drive back to London from the training camp facilitated the flooding in of one memory after another.

"Ronald, you didn't have to come back, we were happy and Max was thriving." My mother never usually shouted but she spat these words out with considerable force.

"Firstly, I had to get you away from him and secondly I have to help our armed forces."

My father who would normally shout said this quietly. Max slowly got out of bed hugging, his by now cold water-bottle but his fever now sustained him protecting him from the cold as he pressed an ear to the door.

"Firstly, he was no threat to our relationship just a bit of fun and secondly you build bridges, you don't blow them up." My mother always had an answer!

"Firstly, he was black and secondly in order to blow up a bridge you need to know its features and weaknesses," my father sounded more confident.

"He wasn't black he was brown and can't they use drawings to find weaknesses?"

"He was more black than brown and they need someone to interpret the drawings if they can be found." My father was winning.

"You could have left us there." My mother seemed very upset, she could have been crying.

"No, people were beginning to talk and Max is going to prep school. I have an important appointment. Look after your son." The conversation was over and at this point I ran out and rushed into my mother's arms. She was crying and I was crying, my father looked on with disgust and left.

"What's prep school?" I asked.

"It's a ghastly place and you won't be going."

"So, can we go back to Cuba?"

"No, maybe, but we are going to go somewhere, not Cuba, near Cuba perhaps, don't worry my darling, I will figure this out."

"When, Mummy?"

"As soon as you are over this cold, I will have worked something out, so back to bed and get well."

And she did work it out.

The thought of returning home to his wife and children didn't seem so uncomfortable the closer he got to London. The memory of the holiday was pleasant enough. Italy was his wife's choice. She always made the arrangements fearing that if she left the matter to Max they would never get away at all. Two weeks in Puglia, a little known region in southern Italy where some of the beaches reminded you of more exotic places like the Maldives or Mauritius. Through a friend, Alice, his wife had managed to rent a villa with a pool where the children were content. His eldest daughter, Alex who was thirteen was bribed to supervise her siblings and that enabled Max and his wife to relax by the pool with little to worry about except Max was restless, in love with another woman and finding it difficult to please his wife. She seemed contented enough with once a week at home while he was working but her expectations were higher now they were on holiday. Luckily, he developed food poisoning from the fish and used that as an excuse. Then his wife got sunburnt and couldn't be touched. Then one evening little Peter ate something in the local restaurant that brought on a cough that developed within seconds to choking. He had eaten something he couldn't swallow. Max rose swiftly from the table and performed the Heimlich manoeuvre with the skill required to save his son. The other diners rose to their feet and applauded. Not Alice who seemed to blame her husband and after that incident she became an over-protective mother not just with Peter but with the girls as well. So, on their return it still ended up being once a week. She was often too stressed or too tired and as he drove into his drive in North London he smiled to himself without Natalie it could be more but he somehow doubted it.

"Hello darling, look what I just found." Alice seemed in a good mood.

It was an old photograph he thought he had lost. It was a black and white photo of his father and mother on their wedding day. She was as tall as he was. On the back it said Mr and Mrs Hulme and the date. It must have been in his mother's file, which he had removed and kept but hadn't taken very good care of.

"Your mother was quite a beauty. I'm sorry I never met her."

"You wouldn't have got on. Where are the kids?"

"I've organised everything, you're not to worry."

"I'm not worried just tired so I'm going for a sleep."

"So am I. It's been too long, my gorgeous husband."

He hated it when she tried to make herself sexy. It had worked in the past he supposed it would work again. As he climbed the stairs thinking of Natalie he convinced himself that until he was sure about his love for her he had his obligations to his wife. She was right behind him and as she slipped her hand into his he felt an old excitement.

The Real Training

Natalie had not thought that the real training would begin as soon as they arrived. She had planned on a coffee, maybe a short sleep, maybe a hot bath, time to unpack but together with Hans she was herded into a small room where a projector was showing the news from last summer when three black men took nine hostages in the Knightsbridge Spaghetti House. Four hundred officers were deployed and there they remained for five days. Apparently, it was only meant to be a robbery according to police and officialdom but the men put out a statement that they were members of The Black Liberation Army but this was disputed by the then commissioner of police Sir Robert Mark. Natalie felt a lack of interest that even she herself was surprised by.

The man giving the commentary fired a question at a short man sitting in the front row. She didn't hear the answer but the lecturer ignored it anyway. There couldn't have been more than seven people in the room but there appeared to be at least ten rows of chairs. Natalie hated lectures and hoped to be invisible in the back row. She did this frequently at school staff meetings and it usually worked very well, she even managed to get some marking done, not that she had much in her subject. But she found herself next to a man whose body language indicated he was about to ask a question.

"Why do you think the police wanted this played down?" The lecturer took off his glasses and cleaned them whilst waiting for an answer. There wasn't one. The room was silent.

Oh god, thought Natalie, *he's going to ask me to answer it. Why does this always happen to me?* At school it was just the same, teachers would ask her when no answers were forthcoming knowing she knew the answer. Natalie's policy in recent years was to get in first. In her view it was the only way to build confidence and you couldn't be compared to anyone else that way. This worked a treat in her drama classes with shy or unwilling students. It didn't always go so well for her but she knew it was the only way, speak now or forever hold your peace.

She piped up during the pause, "Covering up the truth is always the way with the police." Natalie was pleased with her answer even when everyone laughed she felt she had made her mark. The man put his glasses back on and focussed his attention on her.

"In your opinion was there a justification for not telling the truth?" The lecturer walked slowly to the back of the room. He appeared to be looking at her legs.

"If you stop looking at my legs I will try and answer." Everyone laughed even more. This time he was looking at her directly and chose not to respond. Natalie plunged in with her answer.

"In the current climate of racial tension, both in this country and around the world, the police might want to keep things calm." She was proud of this comment and no one laughed this time.

"Are you suggesting that because it's so hot this summer we should expect riots from our black communities?"

Natalie could feel a put-in-your-place moment if it hadn't already happened so she sidled out of answering by suggesting he might like to be more inclusive and ask someone else. Instead he asked another question and looked to Hans for the answer.

"Do you think this incident was handled well?"

Hans replied, "I wasn't there so the only way I can judge is by the outcome and that was as good as it could be, no one was killed, the perpetrators were captured and put in prison."

"A good answer, young man."

Yes, thought Natalie, *there it was, the put down.*

Back in the hut they were sharing, Hans watched Natalie undress in front of him. What was she thinking? It made him nervous; he knew any desire for her would never come to anything. In fact, Natalie had undressed without thinking, she was thinking but about Max. She blushed when she noticed Hans looking at her and apologised and retreated to the bathroom.

"It's OK Natalie," he shouted after her.

"I know you're out of bounds even if I did find you desirable."

Natalie came out with a small white towel around her, which is all that was supplied. It barely covered her body. She sat on the single bed, which she had dumped her one suitcase on and looked at him properly perhaps for the first time.

"What do you mean?"

"You and Max, it's obvious to me anyway." Hans looked down at the floor.

"Tell me about him, about his family and don't spare my feelings."

"I only know he has a wife and three children."

Natalie already knew this but couldn't help the way this information gripped her throat and seemed to sear through her body making her collapse onto the bed losing all sense of dignity. Without moving she pressed on with more questions

"What are their names? What is her name?"

"Alice."

"And the children's names?"

"Peter, Alex and Sophia," he said rather reluctantly.

There was a knock on the door that they had left open to try and keep cool in the late afternoon sun.

"Good afternoon, my name is Adam, we are scheduled for a training session at 5.00 pm depending on how hot it is so you might want to come to the canteen for something to eat before the session."

"I thought we might just relax for the rest of the day," Natalie said, her voice trembling not yet recovered from the shock of the reality of Max's family.

"Afraid not." Adam had gone as quickly as he arrived.

"No point in having a shower then." Natalie got dressed in front of Hans and this time he wasn't embarrassed.

That evening in the open air Natalie experienced the pleasure of running, sweating and feeling her lungs might survive the twenty cigarettes she had smoked for the last four years. Her substantial breasts were not really suited to this kind of activity but she even enjoyed that feeling of them protesting every now and again. Before she set off she had been given a sports bra, not pretty but comfortable and after the run that was a least an hour through woods, by streams and even uphill she felt the high, the sense of well-being, and had to agree all the propaganda about exercise was true. And she slept well without anxiety, without any dread of the decision she had made.

Adam woke them up early. He looked about fifty to Natalie, quite short and broad like a square. He smiled at her, she knew he liked her and when he approached the bed she allowed him to uncover her as he had Hans a moment earlier. She was prepared for this intrusion into privacy so she already had her pants and bra on.

"Good, you are almost ready for your next run before breakfast."

"Is there a schedule?" she asked.

"No," replied Adam. "You will be told what is happening the minute before it happens, if you are lucky."

"Come on, Hans."

"I'm right behind you." He emerged from the bathroom.

Natalie had always hated sport of any kind, hating rules, hating competitiveness but this was different. This running business was for yourself, benefitting you and you alone. The competition was with yourself; you set your own goals, your own challenges. No one was watching or telling you to try harder, no one was telling you how useless you were. Your head may have started out full of thoughts and negativity but very soon your head was empty and your lungs were full of oxygen and when you finished you felt indestructible.

When she returned to the hut, Hans welcomed her with a smile. He had beaten her to the end but he was an expert already and had always impressed her with his six-pack.

"When did you get so fit?" she asked wiping the sweat off her face with a small flannel grabbed from the small shower room

"As a kid, my father drilled it into me, we used to march round our small garden before we hiked out into the Black Forrest."

"Was he a Nazi, your father?" Natalie surprised herself, with this question, it somehow just slipped out

"They all were," Hans replied and looked away.

"I mean how committed was he? Or did he just go along with it."

"You mean did he believe the Nazis were right?"

"Yes."

"We never spoke about it."

Natalie was disappointed, having broached the subject, she wanted to know more.

Over breakfast they saw the others again, the small group that they first saw in the lecture room. The lecturer she had taken an instant dislike was there and seemed to be holding court. He was a tall bespectacled man with greased back black hair tinged around the edges with silver strands. He was talking loudly about the GDR's success in Montreal, for swimming, Natalie didn't catch the name of the athlete. She sat down and tried to ascertain whom she might befriend from the group. There was only one other woman. She was older, in her thirties, called Karen. They had exchanged names. There were three other men apart from Hans all young, in their twenties just out of university, all with upper class accents but mustn't hold that against them, she smiled to herself.

"What are you smiling about?" Hans didn't miss anything.

"Nothing, get on with your breakfast." She smiled at him.

Adam sat down between them on the wooden bench

"Why aren't you sitting with the others?" Adam had a high-pitched voice that didn't suit his square muscular body.

"We prefer our own company." Natalie sounded sharp without meaning to.

"Is it necessary?" Hans asked.

"You mean are they with you on your mission, no but you can learn from each other."

He stood up moved into the centre of the small, already stifling canteen and announced the activity after breakfast would be an archery competition and they should be outside ready having chosen teams in ten minutes.

Bastard, thought Natalie, *he's going to make us mix.*

"Why archery?" asked Hans.

"No idea, just as well I was good at darts." Natalie smiled.

She stood up and called out the number one. At first the others looked blank then the other woman shouted two, then another one until two teams of three people had formed.

The contest started at 9 am in a temperature of 70 degrees and by the time it had finished the temperature had risen to 85 degrees Fahrenheit. It wasn't clear who the winners were but everyone retreated to their own huts for shade. Adam would announce the winning team at lunch. Natalie had enjoyed the experience but wondered what it had to do with the mission ahead and with these thoughts she dosed off.

Max got to his office in Gower Street early afternoon. He appreciated the dark wooden panels that created an illusion of coolness. It wasn't at all stuffy and contrary to his memory of his heavy oak desk today it was not at all oppressive but cool to the touch and comfortable to sit at. Yet his powers of concentration failed him. He looked at the framed photo of his wife and children, then the photo of his mother, then out of the window at the parched tree, the hot, shiny pavement, the people in shorts and sleeveless tops. He sat down on the leather chair there as a result of his predecessor's extravagance. It was beautifully cool and comfortable and he found himself dosing, he was tired after his long drive and a feeling of guilt after enjoying sex with his wife and caused a virtually sleepless night. He questioned himself again as to why he hadn't removed the photo of his mother and put it away at least in the drawer.

***

"OK darling, you have been asleep but we have arrived, wake up."

"Where are we, Mum?" I asked.

"Where would you like to be?"

"In Cuba," I replied.

She smiled and said, "As close as it could be, Miami."

"Oh, that is good, just a few miles then."

"Exactly, so Max, a few weeks and then we'll return." She put her arm around me and kissed the top of my head.

"We are going to be picked up by a friend, a man called Malcolm, is that OK, darling?"

I couldn't figure out why it wouldn't be but I do remember when he kissed my mother and it seemed a little too passionate for friendship. That evening when I was put to bed when I wasn't in the least bit tired I couldn't sleep because of the noise they were making. Malcolm's home was huge. It was on Collins Avenue the road that ran alongside Miami south beach next to some fancy hotels, it was so big I thought it was a hotel. When the noises had stopped I got up and walked right from the top floor where I was, down to the second floor where Mummy was all the way tip toeing on cool marble tiles knocking into exotic palms, all familiar from the gardens of Cuba. There were colourful rugs patterned with exotic birds small and large. The wooden shutters were open to the sea breeze and the scents of flowers were mixing with smells of cooking coming from the basement where the kitchen was. There was very little furniture in the house, was it to be our new home? I so wished it.

"What yer doing wondering around little mister?" A small and very smiley black lady appeared.

"I couldn't sleep, I don't know the time."

"It's surely past your bedtime—nine in the evening," she said.

"What's your name and why are you cooking so late?"

"I'm cooking for the boss and your mum when they get up."

"Why are they in bed?"

She didn't answer but introduced herself as Bella and Bella became a best friend and played the part of a mum whenever Rebecca, my mother went away which turned out to be most of the time.

***

"Max, wake up, Christ you've just come back from holiday and you're fast asleep."

"Give me a break, Tom. I drove from Gatwick to Wales and back here, and it's fucking hot."

"Well there's a meeting in twenty minutes about the operation." Tom coughed, he was a heavy smoker.

"Has it got a name yet?"

"Err yea." He looked at the file he was carrying – "Operation Baal."

"What?"

"Brecht's first play, I believe." Tom coughed.

"That won't do." Max, noticed how the office now reeked of tobacco.

"It'll have to for now." Tom coughed again. The corridor they walked down was usually dark and damp and very cold but today it felt cool and exceptionally welcoming. Half way down the corridor they stopped at the ancient toilet with a stained urinal that was particularly smelly but both men failed to comment on it as they urinated. Both men looked at themselves in the mirror. Max's dark good looks contrasted with Tom's fair and freckled complexion. They both wore their hair fashionably long; Max's was slightly wavy while Tom's was ginger and curly.

"No wonder they don't let me out of the office," Tom joked. "You're the good looking one who always gets the girl."

"I'm a happily married man, she had to be groomed, and you know the routine."

Tom knew that would be as much information he would get out of Max but everyone had noticed Max had changed. He was edgy, moody, critical, unsettled in some way.

"Where can I get a drink of water in this building?" Max spoke sharply.

"The boss has got that organised, there'll be plenty in his office."

"No ice though?" Max joked.

"Christ, Max, you work for MI5 not the CIA." Tom knocked and they both entered the boss's office.

On the large oval table always covered by a lurid green tablecloth was a map of East Berlin. Max headed straight to the jug of luke-warm water and poured himself a glass.

"Just let me know if you need anything stronger Max and welcome back, good break I hope."

Max nodded. It had been a busy year for the boss and it was unusual for him to be at such a meeting, Max felt almost flattered if a little nervous. He hadn't really made much progress and had decided to use the next couple of months while Natalie trained to put the plan in proper shape. He was relieved when the boss said, "Well I just wanted to wish you luck with Operation Baal. By the way, where did that name come from?"

"Don't worry, we'll be changing that by the next meeting." Max smiled,

"No need to on my account. Well I'm back to that case. What else?"

The boss left. He was referring to Harold Wilson's accusations against MI5. Having resigned in March, Wilson didn't go quietly stating that the agency had bullied him on behalf of the establishment who were trying to ruin Britain's democracy. Max wasn't particularly trained or interested in that style of operation, he always preferred the Cold War option and particularly as he had a personal friend involved, the asset that had vanished was his childhood friend Pablo.

His mother had virtually adopted him as her own son and in the garden of his mother's lover they had played watched over by Bella.

***

"Come on in now boys I have some cooling down drink and some filling up food and then you sleep like the babies you are and if you don't come in now I will squash your beautiful faces into my beautiful bosoms."

"Let's hide." Pablo giggled; he was far too fair for a Cuban, Max thought every time he looked at him.

"That's because you like your mother's breasts."

"So do you, I see you looking."

"And I see you listening, that's private, that stuff."

"Shut up it's my mother not yours."

"Come on, Max, try and concentrate, will you?" Tom sounded weary.

"I can't. Besides, you know the area better than I do, you know who to contact and where to look. I haven't been to East Germany for years now."

"Not the point Max, it's you that has to guide them. It's your operation, she's your responsibility."

"All you have to do is plan a route from the hotel to the East then to the theatre then to the safe house – I'll do the rest. I'm going home now. I'll be in tomorrow at dawn if you like."

But Max didn't go home; he made a phone call from their café in Soho near the wig shop.

The pressure to talk to her was overwhelming and he listened as she told him about the activities and standing naked in front of Hans. This didn't please him but the sound of her voice did and knowing she was coping alleviated some of the guilt he felt about drawing her into his world. He would like to have been there to witness her successes and help her through her failures. His mother would have approved of her.

"Mother, when are we going to live in Cuba? Haven't you finished looking for a house yet?"

"When the war is over, another year or so, besides you need to perfect your Spanish first."

"Will he come as well?"

"Pablo? Of course, he's the only brother you'll ever have."

"No, I meant your lover."

Mother slapped me and then cried all over me saying, "Sorry, sorry, sorry."

I didn't have a clue what was happening or what it all meant.

She was true to her word. We left Miami, arrived in Havana Cuba on December 1945.

Our home was smaller but still exuding wealth and power, with two large floors, four bedrooms, three bathrooms and a basement that was off limits to Pablo and me.

The garden was a haven of plants, flowers, and exotic birds brightly coloured and noisy day and night. I loved this new home nearly as much as my mother.

The first evening we arrived, a man arrived with Christmas presents for all of us including Bella. He must have been handsome because Bella said so and I tended to believe everything she said. According to her he was younger than my mother and just a friend who had helped her find a new home. But when the noises that I had come to recognise started in my mother's bedroom I ran to Bella and accused her of lying. She looked sad as I screamed at her and even though she said sorry, I could never trust her again.

Pablo thought I was being ridiculous.

"Your mother is too young to give up on love," he said, "now go and apologise to Bella, she thought she was protecting you."

I did apologise and my eyes were now open so I actually felt grateful, a sense of relief.

My mother was human not some goddess I felt I had to adore even when she deserted us for months on end. Maybe I could stop missing her so much.

***

Max ordered a whisky. God, he felt lonely. It helped to think of his children. He was particularly fond of his first daughter Alex. She was a beauty and reminded him of his mother Rebecca, spirited, always laughing. `He liked his son Peter, but he was closer to his mother; then there was little Sophia who was a mistake. He felt ashamed of how Sophia came about, a drunken man not waiting till his wife was awake enough to say no. Strangely enough Alice didn't mind having another child and she spoiled Sophia so he spoiled Alex and Peter, just fitted in as middle children often do. Max wouldn't send him to private school. Peter wasn't bright enough or strong enough for those battles.

Further Real Training

"It hasn't rained since March," the lecturer stated without emotion. Natalie didn't want to know his name but he addressed his next question to her by name,

"Natalie, can you remember what happened in March?" He was picking on her again, "In terms of current events I mean."

"I know what you meant, Wilson resigned, Peron was deposed by a military coup, Princess Margaret separated from her husband. That's all I can recall."

"Very good, and what about July? Apart from Southend Pier catching fire."

Her mind went blank but this time he was looking at the other woman Karen but before she could say anything, he flashed up on his small rather dirty projector screen in capital letters the word:

ENTEBBE.

Everyone groaned.

"Yes, that not so old chestnut again!" The lecturer laughed.

"What do we know? What do we want to know? What can we learn from the event?"

"I am going to divide you up into three groups and each of you will tackle one of these three questions." Natalie found herself with the least interesting question but the most interesting group. She had momentarily thought it surprising that the intelligence services had ever heard of group work, certainly from her experience of education, it appeared that no one had! Technically speaking it turned out to be pair work except for her group as the lecturer joined her, which was a pity as she had hoped to become better acquainted with the best-looking man she had seen in a long time, apart from Max of course. He had just introduced himself to her as Steve when the lecturer sat beside him.

"So, you have the most challenging question," the lecturer smiled.

"Yes," Steve agreed.

"Why?" Natalie had become fearless in the lecturer's presence, "It seems to me we can't answer we have the media's version of the events but not the facts, we don't have the information required."

"That's true," the lecturer agreed, "but that's the whole point of the exercise, we have to make judgements from the little we know in order to plan our strategy."

Natalie liked the answer; it didn't make her feel out of her depth, and for the first time she warmed to him.

"Can I suggest we wait to hear what the other two groups say and then have some suggestions based on the information they give us."

"A good plan, Natalie, I like your approach," he said it in a genuine tone. She didn't feel patronised.

It became a fascinating afternoon – the others knew a great deal about Entebbe, she came to realise how her job as teacher had led to an insular view of the world, nothing but children, problems with children, problems with children's demanding parents. Teaching was a small world, however rewarding, however amusing, however exciting it was never about the outside world. So as planned, the knowledgeable groups went first and then Natalie was asked again,

"So, Natalie's group, what can we learn from the event?" The lecturer took off his glasses.

"Don't upset the Israelis?" Natalie said with a smile and shrug of the shoulders.

As the morning truck arrived with the daily water ration, Natalie was listening to the small transistor radio on the bedside table. There was no grass left for the cows, so the winter-feed was being used to keep them alive.

Even less amusing according to the news was that the so called Drought Enquiry Office had only got two telephones. The request to use only one bucket of water a day per family couldn't be monitored or enforced so it was a ridiculous edict and no one seemed to know where it had come from. As usual, the country was useless at dealing with extreme weather. In protest she would shower as always after her run and circuit training. A special programme to increase her physical strength had been devised by Adam whose only answer to her question about its relevance to her mission was: "In case you have to climb over walls."

She momentarily wondered what he knew about the mission but then everyone was obsessed with The Cold War so it was an obvious thing to say and the other place there seemed to be a wall was Ulster where if there wasn't a wall there ought to be.

After the shower that day she enjoyed herself exploring different disguises. She refused to use any kind of mask but was becoming skilful at the use of make-up combined with wigs. They didn't have as many as she had left behind at school and many of them were for considerably older agents. She was attracted to a long light brown wig that was reminiscent of her own hair when it was much longer. It was a shade or two lighter but thick and wavy like her own had been before she adopted the shorter style. The disastrous blonde colour had diminished and with it unwanted male attention. The hunt for the most appropriate wig had left her exhausted as she sweated considerably in the heat. She almost looked forward to the afternoon lecture about the mass surveillance techniques of the Stasi intelligence agency of East Germany but after lunch she crept back first to her hut to lie down and regain some energy. On arriving back, she couldn't believe her eyes. It was Max.

Hans had left them alone and went to what was laughingly called the library. It was certainly a quiet hut. Away from the other huts with only a few books intended to take their minds off their training. He found himself looking through a book of photographs. They were landscapes that could have been anywhere, all in black and white, all large and uninspiring except for one photograph that reminded him of home. He had left home to attend Berlin University but on meeting Max or rather Max recruiting him he was sent to study at Cambridge leaving his mother and father alone to deal with their joint guilt. He had decided at an early age he wanted no part of the repressive nature of life in West Germany. His mother and father had been Nazis. As an enquiring child he had always asked questions but when the answers didn't come his frustration turned to resentment. He was clever but not clever enough to stay off the history of Germany. The education system appeared to be in denial as much as his own parents appeared to be. In his small cluttered house on the edge of Freiberg there were no photographs of grandparents or aunts or uncles. It was just the three of them – he often wondered as a child if he was actually theirs. As an adult he had learned the truth. He was grateful to Max when he brought him to Cambridge as his research assistant.

Hans was surprised to see Natalie already seated ready for the lecture. He thought she'd be late, he thought she would be dosing after her visit but she was there alert and seemingly keen. She smiled, she seemed very happy. She looked lovely, slim, healthy and tanned. He was becoming fond of her. She was mature and had the right combination of scepticism and cynicism. He was starting to believe he could trust her.

"Does he like the short hair?" He sat down next to her and she smiled. "Oh yes."

"So," said the lecturer looking straight at them, "What do we know about The Stasi?"

Before anyone could reply the lecturer continued, "*Staatssicherheit*, literally means state security. Its motto is the Shield and Sword of the party. It officially gained independence from the KGB in 1957 but the KGB still maintains its own agents within the organisation." he went on at some length and when Natalie finally looked at her watch it was 5 in the afternoon, her favourite time, time to herself. But Max's visit had made her agitated and to distract herself, she constantly questioned Hans that evening about his past.

"I've told you they didn't talk about the war, did your parents?"

"No, they barely spoke to each other and when they did, it turned into a row."

"Sum up the Stasi for me Hans?" Natalie spoke quietly.

"Christ! Weren't you listening at all?"

"I switched off, I didn't find all those facts very enlightening but their methods are interesting, don't you think?" Natalie's green almond eyes were gleaming at him. Hans knew when she was happy.

"I don't find torture very interesting," he replied and looked away. He knew what she was talking about; their psychological methods, and their ability to enter the lives of the population through blackmail and false promises was well known; bribes of better and bigger flats to live in if they watched the neighbours and reported anything suspicious.

Hans decided not to engage in conversation with Natalie anymore as he knew all about it from Max. Although he himself hadn't been to East Berlin, Max had many times and never wanted to go back. M15 never sent him back but instead redirected him to the role of handler. Additionally, he was to be their chief recruiter covering Europe and occasionally the Middle East.

He felt much better to have seen her even only for an hour in a hut on a single bed. He smiled as he recalled they ended up on the floor in a new and very undignified position, the thought of someone trying to come in made him laugh out loud. The long drive to London awaited him. Next time, he swore to himself, he would get a train much faster.

***

"Happy 16th my lovely son." All the way from Florida she had come for 24 hours and had brought him a drum kit. "Now you can make all the noise you like, make it with Pablo and have fun my darling." There was a different man with her, he followed her up to her bedroom, Pablo tried to distract him by playing the drums, and he was good at it. Max never touched the drums, he knew he wouldn't be any good at it; instead he went upstairs and listened outside his mother's bedroom. He listened for 30 minutes or more but there were no familiar sounds, there was just whispering and he couldn't understand a word even when the drumming stopped.

"What are you doing?" Pablo whispered.

"Listening, of course."

Pablo tutted and whispered, "If you want to know about sex there are other ways, I will take you to a girl I know who will show you everything."

"No thanks, Pablo, I will find out for myself."

"By listening to your mother? That's horrible."

"What do you think they are doing if not sex?"

Pablo dragged him downstairs by the arm, he was always physically stronger than Max.

"Come outside, we can hunt for some hairy spiders."

"No thanks, I want to know why my mother is never here and when she is, she brings a different man."

"Why are looking at me like that?" Max felt the anger building up, "Well, speak if you've something to say."

Pablo spoke hesitantly "It's only a theory."

"What is? If it's about my mother you should tell me." Max felt tears forming

Pablo breathed in deeply. "I think your mother is a spy."

Interrogations

Max didn't like watching interrogations even behind glass in a separate room. He often switched the sound off to help him but then when he couldn't follow the proceedings he would tune in again but would then have to turn his back on the visual. Over time he made a discovery that by being focussed on the visual without sound he could read the body language of both the prisoner and the interrogator more clearly and then by switching just to vocals and then back again to visual he could tell whether the interrogator was making any progress and whether the prisoner was telling the truth. Timing was crucial with this personal approach and over the years he refined his technique considering a number of factors. He observed that women prisoners were more guarded with respect to body language almost as if they knew how much could be communicated this way. Male prisoners were more guarded orally and as they over compensated in their voices they neglected their body language. So, he tended to watch the men closely for the signals conveyed through their body language and listen to the women as they revealed more through tone and inflection. He was often proved to be correct with regard to the truthfulness and validity of the outcome of an interrogation. In fact, he was asked to write a paper on his theory and practice but his academic life was over and frankly the idea of writing a paper on it bored the pants off him and he was sure it would everyone else who might take the trouble to read it.

When it came to watching Natalie being trained to resist interrogation his theory went out the window. Of course, she would have an even more finely developed sense of communicating though body language that had been an essential feature of her job as a drama teacher. She had no idea he was watching behind the glass and the whole thing was more role –

play than anything else, taking her through the 'what if' scenario. There was also the added complexity of her cover story that was eighty per cent true. She was a drama teacher on secondment doing research on Brecht and his theatre in East Berlin. So, he left the room reluctantly at first because he had such strong feelings mainly protective ones but the room had become so stifling and he felt like an intruder somehow or maybe he just wanted her to succeed without his help.

As a distraction he went across to see Hans. The door to the wooden hut was open but no breeze entered and Hans wasn't there. He lay on Natalie's bed deciding to wait for her return. He had booked himself into the hotel and decided to take her there for the night. He had left London that morning to escape the heat or that's what he told himself but he couldn't bring himself to concentrate on the final details of the plan besides Tom was able enough. The stifling wooden hut was unbearable but neither Natalie nor Hans had ever complained to him. Staring up at the ceiling he saw webs that indicated fairly large spiders had spent some time there. Spiders loved heat and responded by growing larger and bigger the hotter it was. He had discovered that to his cost many times in Cuba.

***

"Happy Birthday." Pablo gave him a gold watch, Max was more embarrassed than shocked.

"How could you afford this?"

"I saved up – 21 is a special one with the English isn't it?"

"Well yes, but…"

"Darling," there she was, his mother, on cue, this time without a man.

"Pack a suitcase we are going on a celebration trip."

"Where to?"

"It's a surprise Max." He loved how theatrical she was.

A cab picked them up and by the time the plane took off, it was dark.

"Where are we going, Mother?"

"Close your eyes and I will tell you when to open them."

It was a very short plane journey.

He woke up with her kisses and her smile.

"Stop, we're not staying – we are going to the hotel."

"Great, I need a bath."

Max smiled and they both left without waiting to see Hans.

In the car he couldn't keep his hands off her thighs even at the barrier – even when the soldiers looked and laughed. He was losing his sense of reality let alone dignity and he couldn't care less.

He felt playful but after her bath, Natalie fell asleep. She had after all been through an interrogation and some pretty energetic sex. But as soon as he moved off the bed she woke up and with a scared voice she asked, "Am I really going to be interrogated?"

"Of course not, and even if you are your cover story is real except for a few minor details."

Not convinced, Natalie continued, "What if we don't find your asset?"

"Then you return."

"And go back to my job?"

"If you want to."

"And will I ever see you again?"

"If that's what you want."

She decided to ignore his casual approach to her questions. She sat up in the bed but felt the need to cover herself…

"What do I do if Hans is taken and interrogated?" She grabbed his arm.

"You come home."

"Will you come and get me?" He didn't answer. He even looked away.

"You're a little short on detail Max and you could be more reassuring."

"I brought you here so we could relax and you could unwind. The interrogations are going to get worse and then you will learn how to kill people, and then you will go into the field and it will be real."

She knew that was the end of that particular discussion. It was the way he pursed his lips together as if he was about to blow someone a kiss and then stretched his lips as if he was about to smile. Neither of those things happened.

Max had always loved Miami. His mother wanted him to celebrate his birthday in a luxury room in an art deco hotel on Miami south beach. His mother had provided him with what he could only imagine was a high-class call girl. Had she thought he was a virgin? Surely, she had realised Pablo had sorted him out many years before. The girl left before he could thank her and his mother swanned in as if nothing had happened.

"As you're not ready to go shopping, I'm taking Pablo to go with me. We'll see you later."

That was fine with him. He wanted time alone. He went to the pool and swam for a good thirty minutes. He then walked through the tiny wooden gate that led to a wide sandy beach and the sea. There was nothing on it except him and he lay on the sand looking at the sky and thinking about his future. He had done nothing with his past; he was little more than a playboy in his mother's house in Havana. He learned Spanish then German then French then how to read music, then how to play it on a piano. Then he learned to drink and smoke and gamble.

"I'm not going back to Cuba," was all he could think of saying as he quite by accident walked into the wrong room. They hadn't gone shopping.

"You can't live with me Max; my job doesn't allow it." She lay on the bed naked.

He tried to ignore what he had just discovered and although his mother was comfortable with that, Pablo didn't know where to look.

"And what is your job, screwing young men?" He turned back from looking towards the window as he heard the rustle of her covering her body.

She didn't answer.

"How long have you two been at it?"

Pablo walked across the room and put a towel around his naked body, went into the bathroom and his mother continued to ignore his question. She lit a cigarette.

"I'm getting dressed now and I'd rather you left my room."

"Before I do, I want to know what it is that you do here in America and don't lie."

"Max, it's too dangerous for you to know."

"Well, let me guess you are a spy. Pablo told me years ago, that's fine with me and why it had to be a secret all this time, I don't know. Aren't you supposed to tell your next of kin?"

"I'm not telling you anything; I'm not confirming anything."

"I'll see you both at dinner then?" Max was desperate for a drink.

Max went straight to the bar and started on whisky. Pablo was already there

"Max, I should have told you."

"How long has this been going on, the sex I mean?"

"Since we started to work together about two years ago."

"You mean spying, and don't you treat me like she does, denying everything."

"Yes, we work together; we work well together."

Max could only sneer and order more to drink.

The barman stayed too long pouring the drink.

"Get lost, will you?" Pablo took his arm and manoeuvred him to a small table in the corner of the bar.

"Max, please try not to be so angry. It became too dangerous for your mother to work alone. It always works better as a couple."

"Spying!"

"Yes, and try to keep your voice down."

***

"Before I go to East Berlin, can we talk about your family? In case I don't come back." Natalie was being serious.

"Don't be so dramatic, and we can talk about them any time you like."

"Was your mother a spy?"

"Oh yes, but I thought you meant my current family. I have a wife and three children."

"I know, Hans told me."

"Do you still love her?"

"My mother yes, my wife no."

"I'm glad it's that way round."

"How many lovers have you had apart from me?"

"Not that many and never like this."

"Is your mother still alive?"

"Kind of, she's incarcerated in an American prison."

"For being a spy?" Natalie was genuinely shocked.

"Yes, but for the wrong side."

***

Pablo was so evasive that night and when his mother came down to dinner Max couldn't handle the two of them together and took himself off angry and upset but on a mission to make sense or more sense of what he had discovered that day. It didn't take long. He started in Pablo's bedroom that clearly hadn't been slept in. It took him all of ten minutes to find evidence of spying. There was the false passport; there was a code-book and a gun. In his mother's room that still smelt of sexual activity he found photographs of Cape Canaveral under the mattress, her negligence overwhelmed him with disgust. He wasn't sure whether he was disgusted with the nature of her deceit regarding his best friend or the fact she was working as a spy or that she might have been working for the enemy.

He became filled with a sense of self-loathing. How had he missed it all? He returned to his room packed his bag, walked quickly down to the foyer and booked a cab to the airport. He would decide when he was at the airport where he would go. He had his passport and money that's all he needed to leave the life behind. He felt better as he persuaded himself to get the very next plane out of the US. He looked at the board and saw a flight to London that was already boarding. And yes, there was a seat. He had never been this spontaneous in his entire life but he had to remove himself from the situation if only to comprehend what he had witnessed in the last twenty-four hours.

But then it wasn't that spontaneous. He was English after all; perhaps he was just going home.

***

Hans returned from the interrogation hut shaking.

"What's the matter with you?" Natalie asked in a shocked voice. She touched his forehead, he was hot not the summer heat hot but red-faced, in fact red all over and sweating. She went to unbutton his shirt but he screamed, "Don't touch me!"

"They want you now we can talk later, I'm going for a walk."

"Sure, see you at dinner." But then he turned and spoke more gently.

"Maybe, I may just sleep so don't wake me." He took his shirt off and lay on the narrow, hard bed.

"Would you like some water?" Natalie spoke very quietly. He ignored her and turned to the wall.

Natalie walked to the interrogation hut more concerned about Hans than herself. She was apprehensive now as the mission was fast approaching. It was near the end of training and they might soon be leaving. He was probably just overheating, as the interrogation hut was the hottest hut on the training camp. She tripped slightly over a stone and noticed how the soil blew up like dust on to her sandaled feet. She stopped and noticed how the leaves on the trees were brown and how many of them lay on the ground crispy. She picked up a handful but before she could crunch them in her hands they disintegrated. She saw the hut she shuddered involuntarily.

As she opened the door it was completely dark and out of the dark came the voice that requested her to sit down and take some refreshment. This was not the voice she remembered from the last interrogation. It was intense and uncomfortable. She took the drink of what tasted like lemonade. It felt like being at the dentist, the large comfortable leather chair with the adjacent round shaped extension for the cup. The lemonade relaxed her in some strange way she had never experienced. The command came to drink it all. After what seemed like a long pause but she seemed to have lost all sense of time the voice started the questioning. She lost track of how many questions as they all seemed to roll into one or the same question repeated several times. Was it one question over and over or was it many questions? Was it always the same questions trying to break down her cover story that was her true story or was it the same question? She became confused about her ability to withstand the pressure of this session. She had always been assured no physical pain would be experienced and the reason she was told was that the Stasi wouldn't dare do that to a British citizen.

She was more than ready for the next drink, as her mouth had dried up. This time it was cherry flavoured and cold. There was another pause in the questioning.

Suddenly the voice strapped her into the seat, first the wrists then the ankles. This had happened before and was part of the routine. She didn't feel disconcerted about the different voice now or was it that she no longer heard it as something new was happening. Her head started to spin and she suddenly went dizzy and felt nauseous, then her head started to move in a strange rhythmic way. She started to see in bright eye stinging colours, yellows, greens followed by reds running into whites. She tried to get up, her straps had gone but she couldn't move. It was the floor that was moving, moving away from her. Someone must have switched the light on because she could see the walls of the hut as they began to drip away and when she reached out to touch them, they moved away from her hand. The walls were like waves of different colours again eye-stingily bright changing from white to yellow to purple to black. It was the harshness of the white that hurt her eyes the most and then came the sounds not of waves but heavy bubble-like sounds then high-pitched snappy sounds then sounds that made sense because she had answered them before. They were words formed into questions, questions that she could hear as if they were coming out of a loud speaker but she couldn't hear her answers. She started shouting her answers and she still couldn't hear them.

"I am here to do research for my thesis – I am English – I am a teacher – I am 24 – I am not a virgin – I am not married – I have a lover – His name is Max."

Natalie had collapsed and was carried back to the hut by Adam. Max lifted her out of Adam's arms. The two men had known each other for many years but hardly ever spoken. Max didn't give a second thought to Adam's obvious disapproval of his emotional attachment to Natalie. Max placed her gently on the bed and without a word began to undress her. He swabbed her down with a cool sponge as if she were a child with a fever. She was murmuring but he knew she wouldn't come out of this for several hours and Max wondered if he could stay long enough to see her fully awake. It was already dark but he wanted to be the one to explain. Hans returned with a fresh jug of water.

"I'll make sure she's well hydrated. Max, you should go. I know you will want to explain but perhaps it's better if she thinks you weren't here."

"Should I have prepared her?"

"No, you know it's against the rules and besides that may have made her too anxious. At least now she can tell herself she can withstand the drugs."

"I must get back to London."

"It's OK, Max. I will look after her, after all it will be me in the field with her, not you. It should be me that explains."

He looked at Natalie before leaving he wanted so much to hold her and say he was sorry. As he left he said,

"I'll see you both in London then."

Hans

Natalie slept for twenty-four hours when Hans decided to wake her up. He had washed her down with a sponge at least twice since Max had left and with some of the rationed water from the bucket. The weather was about to change according to experts. They said the rain was coming and more water would become available soon. No one felt optimistic just hot.

She didn't speak and Hans was unsure about how to approach the LSD experience. Like her, he had no idea they would use it as part of their interrogations training but he assumed it was in preparation for what might happen on their mission.

"Fancy a run?" He tried to sound cheerful.

"No, no thank you."

She answered him sweetly enough but turned her head away from him as she slowly got out of bed and went into the bathroom. Max had left her pants on and Hans had seen her naked many times but she suddenly felt ashamed of her body.

She came out wrapped in a towel about ten minutes later. Her face was blank giving him nothing to go on.

"I thought you were going for a run." She smiled weakly.

"Not without you."

"Thanks, Hans."

"For what?"

"Helping me through this. I don't think I made the right decision but it's too late now and besides I might never see Max again if I go back to teaching."

"Natalie, you can leave the service any time you want I can do this mission alone."

"No, I'm scared but committed. Where is Max?"

"He waited as long as he could but he had to return to London, he was sorry because he wanted to debrief you."

"I said his name in the hut."

"That's OK, Natalie, he won't be in danger even if you do say his name. Is that what is worrying you?"

"Of course, suppose I say your name?"

"You better not." Hans liked the fact she was concerned.

Adam interrupted their conversation with the declaration that it was munitions practice phase two. Uncharacteristically he asked Natalie if she felt ready to join them. She ignored his question and simply said with a smile, "How jolly." She had thought of gun practice as she did archery, aim and fire and she was good at it. It would also give her a chance to rebalance herself and feel in control. She never wanted to take drugs ever again whether through choice or force.

The rifle shooting, funnily enough, was on the archery range using the archery targets. But the small arms training took place indoors and this was a noisy and a hot experience. Everyone was groaning. She had been given a small hand-gun, a new pistol designed and made in Czechoslovakia in 1975. It was light and reliable and she had grown quite attached to it. She loaded it and prepared to fire at the picture of a male target but instead turned to Hans who was loading his gun.

"Where were you born?"

Then she fired.

"Berlin."

She fired again.

"When?"

More shots, this time from both of them.

"1946."

She looked at him for a long time – blond with almost, perfect features – he could have been a model. She wondered why it hadn't occurred to her before.

"So, you are older than you look."

Hans laughed.

"If you say so."

***

The lack of photographs bothered him less than the silence. The house was silent, the mealtimes were silent and their lovemaking was silent. He listened very carefully at their bedroom door once a week when it was shut. The only time it was shut. It was always Saturday, always around 10 pm when they thought he was asleep. Ten minutes later the door would be open. Over for another week.

Around the age of fifteen he asked his mother to tell him about her life before his birth and she refused. He waited until both his parents were out and he hunted through the house like a starving animal in search of food. He found her birth certificate in a tatty brown envelope in her underwear drawer. She had been born in Berlin in 1925 so he quickly worked out that she was 21 years old when he was born but he knew that anyway. It wasn't what he was looking for.

***

"Christ! Hans, you're getting worse at this not better. How did you miss him?"

"I'm not really concentrating."

They were out in the open now walking through woods, looking for dummies to appear and kill.

"Remind you of Freiberg?"

"What! This tiny forest? No. The Black Forest is vast and gloomy, full of goblins and demons; princesses trapped in towers. You've had Hans Christian read to you at bedtime, haven't you?"

"Actually no, my parents didn't do that, did yours?"

He ignored her next question. The exercise was paused for a welcome water break.

***

His second search of her room was interrupted by his mother returning home. Full of courage he went down to ask her questions or rather reveal what he had discovered

"So, you were born in Berlin but what about me?"

Like a frightened animal she recoiled from him.

"What have you found?"

"Your birth certificate, and I want to see mine."

"Why, Hans? She went on reluctantly. I can confirm yes, you were born in Berlin in 1946."

"But Father wasn't out of the POW camp yet."

His mother turned pale and collapsed and as he helped her to her bed he knew to leave the subject maybe for another search. She slept but when she woke she called him and revealed her secret.

***

"Sorry, Hans I didn't mean to rattle you."

"Let's sit for a while." He smiled.

The ground was hard, not a blade of green grass anywhere.

"You know Churchill let the Russians go into Berlin first."

"Yes."

"You know why?"

"Well not really," Natalie paused, "well revenge, I suppose."

"Yes, to enable them to get revenge in the most savage way."

"But didn't the Russians suffer more than any other group apart from the Jews?"

"That didn't justify giving them a free reign to do what they did."

She let him continue.

"They raped every woman in Berlin as many times as they wanted."

The silence between them lasted a long time.

"Including your mother?"

"Yes."

"So, you don't know who your father is?"

"Yes, I do, he was one of twenty-five Russian soldiers who raped her that day."

Max had heard from his superior Soames that Natalie had given his name.

"But it doesn't make any difference," he argued, "I'm not going and it's not my code name."

"I repeat, she didn't do well under interrogation." Soames was an ugly short man with a brilliant mind. Max always found it difficult to win an argument with him. Soames' baldhead was sweating profusely in his stifling office.

"Christ, sir, can't you get a fan in here?" Max refused the offer to sit down, as he didn't want to give the impression he was staying.

"It wasn't fair, experimenting on her with LSD."

"It's the latest weapon used by the Stasi."

"What about the money wasted on her training?"

"She's a good shot, she's sharp for a drama teacher and can play any role required," Max persisted.

"And what roles did she play for you…in the boudoir?"

Max hated that word but answered – "Only one, sir, and it was most satisfying."

Soames went red with anger. "Don't be insolent or I'll send you instead of her."

"So, she is going?"

"Yes, get out and get them to Berlin by the end of October and make sure she doesn't fuck up again."

"Would you like me to buy you a fan sir?"

"The shops don't have any left, now get out."

Max drove home to his three bedroomed semi-detached in Finchley where he found his wife alone. They had sex; she got dressed and went to pick up the children from school. He wondered if she knew he was coming home and had planned to look sexy by showing him that she was wearing suspenders. She had crossed her legs slowly enough for him to see. It was quick rushed and in a most inappropriate place. She smiled at him almost smug as if she knew. He began to hate his life, he was not a proper spy anymore, definitely not a proper husband anymore and all he wanted was to be with Natalie. She might not even survive the mission to find Pablo. Christ what a nuisance his childhood companion had become – once a very successful double agent but now with both sides hunting him he had little time left.

***

"Why won't you speak to her?" Pablo was pleading over the phone.

"The same reasons I don't want to speak to you, you're traitors."

"Don't be ridiculous, you lived in Cuba. You could see what the corrupt Americans were doing."

"Not all Americans are Mafia."

"Cuba has the right to self-government by its people."

"Under the rule of the communists?"

"Yes, and those communists will get rid of poverty through free education and healthcare."

"And the ruler of the revolution? What's his name Castro? What will stop him from becoming as corrupt as all men of power do?"

"He's a good man, Max."

"They all start off that way, Pablo. Then they start to like power, money, women and big houses."

"Max, you sound bitter."

"Yes, I can confidently say I am bitter about both of you and by the way are you still lovers?"

"No, that part of my life is over but we are still working together."

"As mother and son?"

Pablo didn't answer.

"Don't phone me again and tell my mother she's lucky to be free of her responsibilities not that she took motherhood all that seriously."

***

His thoughts were broken by the noise of his returning children. They even looked pleased to see him. Too much love in the same day persuaded him he had to stay for dinner that evening. Alex, his eldest naturally soured the atmosphere with her challenging behaviour and inappropriate questions. Sometimes Max thought she could read his mind.

She had never liked Abba but Dancing Queen had been number one for so long she had given up the fight. They played it everywhere and she like everyone else swayed along with the music that invited you to dance with a true love of movement. Her musical tastes included for the most part soul music and anything you could dance to. And she admitted to herself you could dance to this song and it had a story to it.

She was packing for London and hoped that they would leave for Berlin soon after that as she wanted it all over. Hans had retreated from her after their talk. That was the wrong way around wasn't it? They should be closer. Maybe she should have revealed more about herself and family but she thought that would be insensitive and bad timing. His story made her sad.

Filled with self-doubt and a need to be with Max she left the hut for a jog. Exercise was a good idea when you felt out of control of your feelings. She was reminded of the time when she thought of running away from home at the time of her mother's depression. She made it to the local park quite an adventure in her protected world, at least a thirty-minute walk away. She cried without knowing why but jogging today she didn't cry it was a strong deep fear that gripped her.

"Max tells me you are ready for the next stage, the final stage." Soames didn't look up from his desk, "I won't see you again. So, I wish you luck and apart from the final touches here at HQ that I may or may not observe there is no more to say."

"God, he's grim," Natalie smiled at Hans.

Hans broke his silence. "He reminds me of someone."

"Who?"

"My father."

Max came down the dark but refreshingly cool corridor. He wore an open necked shirt and shorts.

"A bit unconventional," remarked Hans.

"No one gives a damn in this heat, not even Her Majesty's Secret Service. Let's all hit the town tonight to celebrate our being reunited." He took hold of Natalie's hand and kissed it softly. He didn't let go until they reached their destination.

They hit Soho big time, Raymond's Revue bar was their first choice but Natalie refused to stay and watch striptease so they progressed to Admiral Duncan's.

"This is tame, let's go to Club Louise." Max had made the decision, rose from the velvet covered armchair and was out the door. They headed to Poland Street, Number 61. It had a red painted door, a gold-plated door knocker. Hans rang the bell and through a little peephole a husky voice said, "Are you members?"

"Yes," Max smiled and the door opened.

Sitting at a low desk in the entrance way was a very old lady with a pile of grey hair loose around her shoulders. She wore a long black dress. "Ah, you, Max where have you been my darling?"

Natalie winced at the false French accent and said before Max could answer, "With me."

"Ah, darling you are so lovely."

All three of them ignored her comment. Natalie giggled.

"Is she the owner?"

"I doubt it, more likely to be a Maltese maniac." Max took her hand again.

They moved into the small foyer that led into a bar room, a large mirror ran along the back wall, very dim lighting so you could hardly see your reflection, long black leatherette sofa seating, small tables with red cloths on them, black chairs, red carpets. Downstairs was the dance floor and Natalie was drunk enough to make full use of it despite the fact she hated Punk music. It was the sort of place you could completely let yourself go without being judged or watched. It made a welcome change from the training camp.

Later the music changed back to the black soul music she wanted to hear.

Wrapped around Max on the dance floor Natalie was experiencing a kind of bliss. Hans remained seated and had no inclination to move from his seat. He drank plenty and watched but Natalie couldn't imagine what he was thinking about.

"You will be safe with him," Max spoke loudly over the music.

"I hope so."

"I think you should dance with him." Max literally put them in each other's arms, ordered them to dance and retreated upstairs. On his return he was surprised to see them still in each other's arms. They make a nice couple he thought. He went over to them and as he separated them he said to Hans, "Stay here, we won't be long."

Madame Louise showed them into a small candle lit room. Afterwards Natalie wondered how many times Max had requested a small candle-lit room from Madame Louise.

Throughout October, Natalie and Hans brushed up on their training. Without the scenic surroundings of Wales, the continuation of training was monotonous and at times disheartening. Shooting practice, being interrogated, learning about The Cold War in HQ was harder even though she was more skilled. And at the end of the day he would be there waiting for her.

On one occasion she noticed Han's facial expression.

"You're jealous!"

"Of course I am, such passion is to be envied."

"Well soon it will just be us two happily married doing research in East Berlin."

"You might need to look a little fonder of me," Natalie teased him.

"I am very fond of you but remember I am German, cold and precise."

"That's very sexy, women like to break that down."

"Stop talking in clichés, you are much more intelligent than that Natalie." Hans was too severe for her mood.

Max was upstairs finalising plans with Tom ready for the chief's approval. They hadn't expected the boss to be so flattering.

"Yes, I am pleasantly surprised, she is good, at some things." Soames smiled. "That was always one of your strengths, the ones you recruited."

"Except for Pablo."

"Well my recollection is your mother did that, you turned him and now we complete the cycle before the Stasi do. Now we can put that right. He can't be allowed his freedom any longer. Take them to the airport first thing tomorrow."

"I'd rather not." Max looked down.

Soames laughed, "Still don't like goodbyes, eh? OK, Tom you need a day out of the office-you look like a mini cab driver. You deliver them to the airport and then take your wife out for a picnic or dinner or shopping."

"Thanks, sir." Tom left the office.

Soames got out of his chair and poured them both whiskies.

"And you Max, how's that marriage of yours?"

"We still have sex, if that's what you want to know."

"Of course you do but does she know about you and Natalie having sex?"

"No, of course she doesn't." Max sipped at the whisky he didn't actually want.

"Natalie may not return."

Max was angry. "She will return even if I have to bring her back myself."

"And then what? Another mission for her?" Soames sounded sceptical.

"I'm not sure she'd want to go back to teaching." Max had calmed down as the whisky kicked in.

"Well go and spend what might be your last night with her." Soames picked up a pen and with a wave of the hand Max was dismissed.

Berlin

Natalie was only half listening more concerned with the strange and unfamiliar noises coming from around the plane. She told herself it must be preparing for the landing but then remembered they had only been in the air for twenty minutes. It was rattling loudly and she decided to put that down to its age. She turned to look at Hans.

"They put it up because they were losing out economically. At first workers just crossed over and returned but then as they recognised the restrictions imposed by the government and so people started to not go back. Many people had crossed for leisure and visiting Brecht's theatre was as common for West Berliners as East Berliners. But it all changed in 1961, starting with a barrier consisting mainly of wire fencing but then came the floodlights, the electric fences, the patrol dogs, the observation towers and armed guards." Natalie smiled and nodded hoping he hadn't realised she wasn't listening properly.

"Hans, why didn't he come to the airport?"

"Weren't you listening to me?"

"Of course I was, but I knew it all anyway."

"So why did you ask me?"

"To take my mind of flying."

"Have some gin and tonic instead."

"OK, if you're buying."

"He doesn't like goodbyes."

"It's not goodbye as far as I'm concerned. He's changed my whole bloody life and he's staying in it."

"I'm sure he intends to."

The airhostess brought the lunch in small tin foil cartons. It would be terrible but Natalie was hungry and needed something to absorb the alcohol, which had gone straight to her head.

"You know, I once applied to be an airhostess with British Airways and they turned me down."

"Why? You're attractive enough."

"Thanks Hans, but they didn't think so."

On arrival at Berlin's Tempelhof Airport, Natalie had got to grips with her nerves partly due to being back on land however when they were met by an elderly man who looked as old as many of her teachers in primary school she almost lost her faith in the mission. Hans picked up on her anxiety that manifested itself in her inability to talk; Hans simply spoke in German thus enabling Natalie to remain voiceless. The man introduced himself as Hermann and all was in place. This thin grey man was their contact and saviour if required. Natalie felt ill at the very thought of having to rely on such a man.

Hans held her hand in the taxi to the hotel and Hermann smiled.

"I understand that you are researching the great Brecht." he said in excellent English.

"Yes," Natalie found her voice again.

"An unusual honeymoon activity."

"Yes," this time Hans answered.

"Perhaps you would like to enjoy tomorrow together unimpeded by scholastic pursuits. Would you like me to organise a walking tour in the East?"

"Yes, that would be perfect," Hans replied on Natalie's behalf.

The hotel room was dark with heavy, lined curtains that draped across a large window, the kind that were difficult to open and close due to lack of care. The bed was small for a double bed. She didn't want to be tempted to find comfort in the arms of Hans or any other man. As if he read her mind, "I can sleep on that rather large armchair if you like?"

"Don't be ridiculous, Hans. Let's eat and have an early night."

Her small suitcase containing seven outfits precisely was sitting on the small double bed that was covered by a floral eiderdown that looked like it needed a good wash.

As she opened her suitcase she admired her organisation of the seven outfits. Her only hope was that it would take less than a week. Her packing technique improved as her mother was no longer available for that particular chore. She could still hear her saying, *"I'll do the packing for you darling."*

She would watch her mother roll all garments neatly enabling twice as much clothing to fit into the suitcase as she herself could have done.

"I learnt this from the army, about the only thing I did learn." Her mother smiled. Pants and socks were stuffed into shoes and toiletries were separated between the layers of clothes. A large plastic bag covered everything and was to be used for the dirty clothes.

"We are only here for a week, Hans?"

"Hopefully."

"I've only packed for a week."

"Well you can either wear everything twice or get them washed."

"By whom?"

"The hotel will do it, Christ you're going to have to iron that lot before you wear it. I thought women knew how to pack a suitcase."

"Should I hang them up?"

"No, we may actually have to move across to the East in a couple of days. I thought you weren't going to wear any wigs."

"I only brought this one to remind me of Max." She noticed Hans smirked at the remark.

At that moment an envelope was pushed under the door. Hans picked it up, got out a copy of Orwell's 1984 and began to decode the message. Such a strange choice to use for decoding Natalie thought to herself but what she didn't know was that it used to be Jane Austen's Emma. She decided against unpacking completely and just chose a brown woollen midi dress to wear for dinner partly because it was on top of her other clothes and partly because the hotel was chilly. It fitted nicely under her well-formed breasts and set off her curvy bottom. She couldn't decide whether to put her hair up in a bun or let it hang loose. It was nearly shoulder length now and her new hairdresser had made a good job of the colour for her complexion, brown with golden highlights.

"What do you think boots or shoes?"

Hans didn't answer. She decided to have a gin and tonic from the mini bar but she couldn't find it and said, "I'm going to the bar I need a gin and tonic."

"Wait."

"But you're not ready."

"Yes, I am, this only tells us the arrangements for the day after tomorrow."

"But you haven't washed or cleaned your teeth."

"I don't need to until I go to bed." Hans was slightly puzzled by the instructions.

"Typical."

"What is?"

"Men, you're all so dirty, unhygienic, smelly," she screwed up her nose.

"Thanks, I get your point." They both laughed. Hans ensured their door was secure, double locking it with the brass key that had the number 200 on the tag. There was no way one would want to carry this object round all day. He placed the thin cotton across the bottom of the door.

"Is that necessary?" Natalie asked. "We are in the West, still though the dinginess of this hotel makes me dubious as to what to expect on the other side."

"Try to keep your voice down," Hans spoke quietly to indicate the level he wanted her to speak at. They got to the lift and were joined by a woman whose hair reminded her of women's hairstyles when she was young in the fifties. Her mother's voice slipped into her head again.

"That bloody beehive has left a grease mark on the wallpaper. She mustn't have washed her hair for a fortnight or was it her boyfriend's greasy hair."

"Must have been 'cause she was sitting on his lap all evening," this Natalie said to her mother in a supportive tone.

"Why she had to come, I really don't know."

"Well, it was a party and she is a neighbour."

"Not anymore, she's left home. I think he was a soldier with that haircut."

"Probably, Mum."

The woman in the lift spoke to Hans who smiled and seemed very relaxed. Natalie couldn't bring herself to smile at a woman who was so completely behind the times. She got out before the ground floor where the dining room was.

"I hope you didn't ask her to join us for dinner."

"No, she was just asking me about our visit."

"What's the food like in Germany?"

"Better than in England even though they lost the war."

They sat down to a meal that she actually enjoyed especially as it was washed down with a bottle of German white. She thought the meat was pork and Hans confirmed that it was an Eintopf—a pork stew with some sort of cream.

"Hans, can I phone Max?"

"No, he will contact us if he needs to. Now, the day after our tour tomorrow we will cross to the East. The message tells us when and where to collect our papers and tickets."

"How do we cross?"

"At Checkpoint Charlie as we are tourists. Then we walk to the theatre and you start your research."

"And what do you do?"

"I keep my eyes open."

"Hans, is this man just going to step out of the shadows and say here I am."

"I doubt that. He is in hiding and he will be afraid but his last known contact was at the theatre, according to one of our agents."

After a dinner they went out for a short walk.

"Why are we in the American sector," she asked Hans

"Because it's more attractive."

"Really?"

"You wait till you see the East!"

"You know David Bowie lives here." Natalie had only recently become a fan.

"Yes, he lives in Schoneberger Haupstrasse."

"Is that close?" Natalie felt quite excited and tucked her arm through his.

"Fairly, but tonight I will show you the source of everyone's angst – the wall."

They turned towards the Brandenburg Gate and there it was the wall that divided the city, cutting across streets and squares. It stood directly on the streets or along rows of houses. It stood directly behind the Reichstag and then went in an arc around the Brandenburg Gate. Natalie was horrified. Hans pointed out a patch of land surrounded by watchtowers.

"That's Potsdamer Platz, it was once the Piccadilly Circus of Berlin."

Goodbyes

Max was in his office and already agitated by 11.00 am. It was cooler now. Autumn well underway and he was happy to be back in trousers. His obsession with Natalie was a constant irritation to him and in her absence, he was ashamed that it became necessary to have sex with his wife in the belief that this would help him put her from his mind and also make it easier never to see her again. She would never make a good spy and Soames had made it clear, she would be signed off on her return. "Put out to pasture," he had joked. Then he got serious,

"Of course, you must never see her again Max, you know that and besides your wife is much more attractive you know. Why you ever stray I don't know."

They had been having a drink at Soames' club the evening before when Soames had made it clear the affair with the teacher was over.

"And don't tell me you love her Max, it's just sex." Max couldn't be bothered to argue with Soames.

The following day as he sat in his office he concluded that Soames must be right and he would fight his feelings. He finished some paperwork and went to get a haircut.

***

Natalie had said she liked men with long hair. It was dark with not a sign of grey but she said she would love him even more with long grey hair. She talked about his body as if she owned it.

"I love the fact you're not too tall."

"Excuse me, I'm five feet ten!" Max exclaimed.

"OK, but I'm five feet six, so that makes you a perfect fit for me. And I like your hairy chest, and I love your legs."

"Women are not supposed to care about these things, you're supposed to love us for our personalities."

"I'm a feminist," Natalie exclaimed.

"Doesn't that mean you don't like men?"

"Not at all, it means we can treat them as sex objects the same way men treat women."

"So that's all I mean to you?"

They had both laughed. He had chosen a good hotel for their last night. The Savoy, the one they went to in the early stage of their relationship. It was anonymous, expensive and she was worth it.

***

"How did you become a spy?"

"When I left Florida and came to London, a man picked me up from Heathrow Airport and offered me a job. I was to go to Cambridge University, study English and spy on a group of communist activists and anyone else they wanted me to."

"Is that where you recruited Hans?"

"It's where we became friends."

"And this man, your asset? Was he at Cambridge?"

"No, I knew him before, and then he became a spy, when I knew him later."

"Did you work with him on something?"

"Yes and no – we were a team for a while, almost brothers."

Natalie knew when he was becoming fed up of her curiosity.

"Thanks Aristos – a little short but I'll get used to it."

***

There was a storm that afternoon. He shuddered and left the barbers. He decided not to go back to the office. He was in the mood for a film. Just to sit and relax, lose himself. There was a new release, an American film, Car Wash, a comedy with music, maybe some social comment on race.

He went in and did indeed lose himself. The music was good, it made him smile. He didn't think too much about the exploitation of Black Americans. He decided to go home and not return to the office. His wife opened the door before he could get his keys out.

"What's the matter?"

"It's Alex, she's been truanting, the school wants us to go in and explain, apologise, or something."

"Can't you deal with this, Alice? I mean you are her mother and you've fuck all else to do."

She slapped his face and he never saw it coming.

"Okay, I will but they wanted to meet her father but I'll explain he's too busy except he wasn't that busy as his boss phoned to ask where he was all afternoon."

"Soames phoned here?"

"Yes, apparently it's important."

On his return to the office Soames kept him waiting. Max was as tired of being lectured about his personal life as he was tired of his personal life. He almost didn't knock. He wanted to pretend he hadn't got the message. But he knew it would be even more difficult to pretend and Soames would guess he had got the message so he did knock and as he walked in he sensed there was a problem from the expression on Soames' normally inexpressive face.

"Where have you been?" Soames asked.

"Just popped out to get a haircut and then I went home to make love to my wife but then she said you wanted me urgently and here I am."

"Yes, now you look more like MI5."

"Well that's what I was going for."

"And the film?"

"Are you having me followed?"

Soames didn't answer.

"What did you want to see me about?"

***

Natalie had insisted Hans slept in the small double bed or was it a large single? They were both chilled from the walk in more ways than one. To see a city divided in two was disturbing and illogical.

Predictably the bed was lumpy and Natalie couldn't help but recall the bed she stayed in with Max only the previous night.

There was no choice, as the mattress also dipped in the middle, but that meant she had to be physically closer to Hans than she wanted to be.

He joked about not being Max and she joked about wishing that he was. She fell asleep with the picture of barbed wire in her head.

On waking Natalie felt bold.

"Why don't you make a pass at me, Hans?"

"I don't find you attractive."

"Thanks, I think I'll have a shower." The water was cold and then thankfully became lukewarm. She welcomed wrapping the towel around her and ensured whilst dressing Hans didn't get a view of skin. Feeling ashamed of her immaturity she sat on the edge of the bed and dried herself slowly wondering how she could regain some dignity with this strange man who had become a friend. But she didn't have to, as she was about to apologise another note was slipped under the door. Hans heard it and went to pick it up. She smiled at him and handed him the code-book from the bedside drawer where she had put it last night. She got dressed as he decoded the message.

"What's the matter?" Natalie saw how he had tensed up.

"The arrangements have changed. We are meeting our contact in Kreuzberg, the artist's quarter, here look at this map and see if you can find this street."

Natalie was useless at map reading. She recalled that passing her O-level geography was totally reliant on glaciation, the only thing she learned and understood. She surprised herself when she found the street immediately and by the time Hans came out of the shower she had drawn up her own route.

"Good work." He smiled. "Let's go."

"What about breakfast? I'm actually very hungry."

"We'll eat there, the place is full of cafes and restaurants."

They waited long beyond breakfast and decided to revert to plan A. Natalie continued to map read and they found their way to The Berliner Ensemble. There was no problem at Checkpoint Charlie, their cover story and their papers worked like a dream.

They spent the remainder of the day in the theatre. They waited, they watched, Natalie took some photographs but as dusk arrived they decided to walk back to the hotel.

Again, there was no problem in getting back to the West side.

"Maybe we should try tomorrow?" Hans said, "Maybe I got the day wrong?"

"OK, we'll go back for breakfast tomorrow." Natalie put her arm through his, she didn't know why. When they arrived at their room there was a third note waiting for them.

***

"Max, go home I will ring you as soon as we have some more information."

"How could it have happened?" Max expressed his astonishment by sitting down as if a cricket ball had hit him in the stomach had hit him.

"The details are hazy but she's all right, some kind of injury, err injuries it's a bit unclear – it's Hans we need to be worried about, he may never recover. You must go and sort this out with as much efficiency you can muster given your emotional involvement." Soames poured himself a whisky and offered Max one.

Max grabbed the glass and saw both his hands shaking as he took it from Soames.

"It's why I didn't want to go in the first place and if I go now I will just shoot him outright."

"Not before you get the information we require from him then you can shoot him but I want to know how he knew they were coming for him. If your mother hadn't been incarcerated in a high security institution in the States, I could almost believe she had something to do with it."

Max held out his empty glass with his hands still shaking and Soames looked at them and then into Max's eyes. His eyebrows were full and dark like Dennis Healy's. What an odd thought to have, Max said to himself as he watched Soames pick up the phone, "Get me Frank across the water. No, not Frank across the Thames, the other Frank across the pond." Soames smiled, "She's a new receptionist, bit slow but rather pretty though. Go home and pack and give my love to your wife. Give her a night to remember you by."

Max finished his whisky with one gulp and resisted the urge to say anything after all Soames had always been crude but as he got up he swore to himself that this was his last mission and he wanted out and he wanted Natalie with him.

His wife was out when he rushed home to pack. That was a relief, no goodbyes, no explanations, and no regrets, apart from the children. With Natalie in danger, hurt somehow, his mind was made up to leave his wife and the service. He'd had enough.

He boarded the plane with one thought in mind, to bring her back safely.

The next morning just like the day before, the street was full of people; young people smiling, smoking, drinking coffee. This was an artist's haven. Some of them were even sketching, others were showing their work and some had placed their work rather haphazardly against the chairs and tables on the street. Natalie was delighted by the colourful fashion on display, the long skirts worn by the women with long plaited hair; the flared trousers worn by men and women, often velvet in different colours. Tapestry waistcoats were also in abundance. No one seemed in a hurry even with empty coffee cups in front of them, they carried on talking, not the English way at all. Hans and Natalie enjoyed their breakfast of bread, ham and cheese with coffee that tasted good, really good. But doubts surfaced even with the sun shining and a great breakfast

"Hans, this just doesn't feel right."

"Just relax, Natalie and trust me. I'm going in to pay the bill, we must be ready to move quickly."

***

Max resisted the alcohol offered by the airhostess. He noticed how attractive she was and she lingered a little too long. It made him uncomfortable. Many women did this and once he was prepared to pursue their interest but today he found it irksome. He turned his head away and looking out the window, he could see they were close to landing. This bit was never enjoyable, too many odd sounds, too much vibration, too little hope if something went wrong. He hoped she was all right. Hans was in a bad way – might never recover – Soames' words kept going through his mind. Natalie had injuries – what did he mean? When he pressed Soames, he wouldn't elaborate.

It was a rough landing.

Part Two

Starting Again

"I don't understand why this took so long." Natalie was putting books on shelves.

"Which part? Leaving the service? My divorce? Getting married again? Raising enough money to buy this place? Getting registered as a detective agency?" Max was putting up shelves but not fast enough to ensure Natalie was kept busy.

"Only you could sum up our romance so unromantically. I need more shelves. Do you really need all these books? You're such a hoarder and we only have one living room, a study and one bedroom. I'm surprised we're not sharing the bathroom with the upstairs lot." Natalie sat down on a pile of books. They smiled at each other.

"Let's explore the pubs round here. Sunday night in the East End, they'll all be up at the mikes imitating 'My Way'." Max had already put down the hammer.

"What about the women?" Natalie glared at him.

"Oh, I expect there'll be up there too doing Shirley Bassey." He kissed her and said sweetly, "I'm going for a shower."

"I'm glad we waited till the spring to move in, don't fancy building shelves by candlelight." Max sipped his lager and felt comfortable in the pub apart from the smoke.

Natalie had taken up smoking again blaming it on the stress experienced in Berlin and all the hardship of Max's divorce both emotional and financial. Her conscience was clear as he had never loved his wife or particularly wanted children. With his share of the house and a package from the service Max could afford a long honeymoon in the Caribbean and a small flat in the East End. The move east to the rather attractive Georgian Square known as Arbour Square was a deliberate choice in the attempt to bring some tranquillity into their lives.

"Darling, if we're as successful as I expect us to be can we move to a two bedroomed flat?" Natalie exhaled her smoke away from Max.

"If we are successful and you give up smoking I'll get you a three-bedroomed flat."

Max managed to cough at the right moment but then kissed her fully on the mouth.

The smoking would never stop him from kissing her. There was singing of the sort she remembered as a child. Frank Sinatra singing 'Under My Skin' and Dinah Washington's 'What a Difference a Day Makes' and then a small blonde woman got up on the stage and sang Dusty Springfield's hit 'The Look of Love', she sang it rather well Natalie thought. Max got up.

"Let's go."

"I'm just getting settled."

"Up early tomorrow, on our first case." Max grabbed her hand.

"When did this happen?" She managed to get her coat on and finish her gin and tonic in one gulp.

"I'll tell you all about in when you're snuggled up in bed."

Max was disappointed with her response to his revelation of their first case.

"That doesn't sound very lucrative." Natalie lit a cigarette; she particularly enjoyed a smoke after sex.

"That's not the point we have to start somewhere and build a reputation, we take anything and everything and we start tomorrow buying a camera as soon as the shops open."

"I've got a camera."

"Not that sort of camera, we need a camera that makes a film to show the client."

"So, we'll need a screen."

"No, we'll just use a sheet for now pinned on the wall of the study."

Natalie frowned, "But how much is this head teacher paying?"

"Depends on the results." She felt tired and a little drunk so she rolled over and waited – he always wrapped himself around her. That was the only way she could get to sleep these days.

Mr Richards the head teacher of a rough and barely functioning school in the East End had seen the small advert in his local paper which he tried to read when he had a spare moment. His secretary always left it on his desk telling him he needed to keep up with local events and then he could impress the parents when he gave speeches. He had never taken her advice because there never seemed anything worthwhile to put in a speech and he had in fact stopped glancing through it some time ago except there was a small part of the paper that advertised everything local from second hand TVs to apprenticeships. He always looked at theses adverts without really knowing why.

He was drawn to one advert in particular

The Versatile Detective Agency

We will solve anything for anybody
No Questions Asked Discretion Assured
Fees negotiable
Phone us on 747-8833

He had never used a detective agency before but his intense curiosity about the nature and extent of the woodwork teacher's sick leave was so obsessing him, he had to discover the truth. But this was a rather unorthodox way of going about things and he wouldn't be able to use the school fund. As he picked up the phone he was a little nervous but relieved when a well-spoken, clearly Oxbridge educated man said, "Good evening, Versatile Detective Agency, how may I help?"

Richards felt awkward but got more relaxed as he listened to the terms and conditions. They didn't even have to meet and the agency would follow and film the teacher to be known as Citizen X. Max had used the title of a film he had seen about a serial killer in Russia, and felt it would be appropriate to use it in their cases, Natalie looked blank as he tried to explain why he found the use of this name amusing. Richards was even more pleased to learn that when the job was done and the evidence provided via a courier he simply had to write a cheque and send it to an address given.

Without consulting anyone, even his wife Millie, he agreed. He was happy the man known as Max promised to start as soon as the details of the case had been delivered.

"Are you sure we have the right address?" Natalie felt chilly in the car even in her winter coat. She often felt cold even when the weather was mild.

Max just pulled a face and didn't answer. The teacher lived in a small terrace house, painted white with a small front garden and a broken gate. They were parked directly across the road. The street was quiet.

"Perhaps he's spotted us and won't come out." Natalie shivered.

"This job takes more patience than you are exhibiting. We've only been here an hour."

Max meant it but said it sweetly enough.

"I'd rather be at home sorting things out. We don't even have the curtains up. Besides this is hardly an inspiring start to our new careers. Who cares about a teacher whose work shy and the money isn't going to pay for a new bed."

"We don't need a new bed Natalie and don't you remember your teaching days and how you were always covering for sick teachers?"

"Yes, I do remember but…"

With a sudden nudge from Max, Natalie had to curtail her demand for a new bed.

"Look, there he is." Citizen X looked just as described by Richards, tall, long light brown hair that often looked dirty. "OK I'll follow him on foot, you drive slowly keeping track of my movements."

Natalie liked driving well enough but not when she didn't know where she was going but she didn't have to worry because Citizen X followed by Max only went as far as the corner shop and bought a paper. She turned the car round and followed them both back to the house. Max got in.

"Looks like more waiting." Max indicated he wanted the driver's seat back.

"Yes, but what are we waiting for?" Natalie moved back into the passenger's seat.

"Some indication that his back problem is not a problem."

98

"Okay," responded Natalie with a hint of mockery in her voice, "but how? Him going to the corner shop to buy a paper proves nothing."

"I've got an idea. I'm going in closer to film him." And without another word Max took the camera from the back seat and crossed the road. He carried the camera on his shoulder, a big, heavy black thing like a large gun barrel. Natalie had used them filming her drama lessons. The department couldn't afford a tripod so shoulder-ache sometimes even backache followed. She wanted to shout after him to mind his back. Watching him through the car window she became frustrated wondering why she was sitting there and missing everything so she did what the service had expected of her and took the initiative. She was after all in disguise. Today she had chosen a red curly wig that sat shoulder length and bright as it was it contrasted well with her black jumper and blue jeans. She wore very large silver hoops in her pierced ears. At first Max was surprised at her crossing the road towards him but when she rang on the doorbell he understood.

The door opened immediately and Citizen X had on navy blue overalls that were splattered with white paint.

"Oh hello, sorry to disturb you but I'm thinking about buying a house in the area and wondered if you could tell me a little bit about it." Natalie wasn't happy with her opening statement but she hadn't prepared for this and she had Max to blame for telling her about their first mission when she was half asleep.

"I'm very happy to tell you anything you want to know. Would you like to come in and I'll make us some coffee." Citizen X seemed nice enough and as Max was tucked round the side pathway she felt safe. Even so it took her by surprise that she felt able to trust a stranger.

"Be careful I'm painting so mind your clothes."

"That's a nice colour you've chosen. What's it called?"

"It's one of those new fancy deluxe whites. The house always felt too dark. My wife liked dark colours you see and now since she's gone I am trying to cheer the place up and me with it," He smiled and continued, "she died of cancer, last week in fact."

"Is that why you're not working?" At this question he stopped smiling and said, "Yes, I've got compassionate leave but only five days."

"Well in that case I should let you get on. Don't worry about the coffee."

Natalie headed back through the front door and wondered if he was lying about his wife. X didn't follow her. Max had got himself into the back garden and had the lens pointing straight at her, which had persuaded her to exit quickly. Her job as decoy was done. Instead of returning to the car, which was in full view from the front window, she took a walk deciding to find out what this part of London was like.

Often enough she had been advised not to wander off after Berlin as it might bring on another episode a sort of nervous breakdown but she was in London starting a new life with the man she loved so what could possibly go wrong.

***

"Hans, are you sure we've done the right thing. The breakfast is lovely but what's to say the third note is genuine and we have always been told to follow the plan."

"The code is correct and plans do change."

Natalie looked across the street and saw the small white van out of which stepped a man with darkish skin, tall and handsome. He looked directly at her and smiled.

Hans stood up immediately and shook the man's hands; they spoke as if they had known each other a long time.

"I have saved you much time, come with me I am ready to be debriefed."

"We are not alone here—" but before Hans could finish his sentence the man interjected,

"You will come with me or you may as well go back."

Natalie realised that this was the man they came for, the double agent, the one they were supposed to bring in. She grabbed Hans' arm but he ignored her and followed the target across the narrow street crammed with cafes. So, in broad daylight they walked into unknown territory. Natalie clung on to Max's words: "Trust him; he knows what he's doing." He told them politely to get in the back and Natalie felt alarmed but Hans merely said, "It's good, he has come to us, and it simplifies everything."

"How? You need to tell me what to do?"

"Be quiet now and wait."

They looked through the small window at the back of the van. The door was of course locked but through the small window they observed the short journey from West to East. Papers were not even checked as the barrier was lifted to allow them through. It was not Checkpoint Charlie but a smaller crossing out beyond the Centre of Berlin. After one hour the van stopped and the asset let them out. They had gone through to East Berlin. When they got out the difference was stark. The buildings were old and, in some cases, almost falling down. There was litter everywhere. There were no cafes or bars visible in this street.

The target seemed cheerful. "Some of us cross through the wall without being checked. This is my home, make yourselves at home while I get us some lunch."

"We're not hungry, we had a late breakfast," Natalie spoke directly to him for the first time. He looked at her long and hard so this was the kind of woman Max loved. He had kept up with every bit of news about his once friend and brother.

"That's OK. I will get us some dinner then." With no warning Pablo drew out a gun and threw Natalie some rope. "Tie him up."

**

Natalie was in a park and breaking out in a panic. She could barely remember the name of the park. She needed to find a sign to remind her of its name. But what did that matter? Its name was irrelevant. The name would not help her to find her way out. She couldn't even find an exit. She had forgotten how parks in London could be that big.

"Shit, I'm lost," she spoke out loud with not a single person around to ask the way. It had already occurred to her that you couldn't walk very far without coming to a tube station. But she was in the middle of a park, how could there be nobody here. Where are the mothers playing with their children? Where are the dog walkers? She sat down with her head spinning. *Please no, I mustn't faint.*

***

He didn't blindfold him while he raped her. He wanted Hans to see so he did it right in front of him. It was violent and sadistic and damaging both physically and mentally.

She passed out and on the occasions she came to, she could hear Hans being interrogated. She couldn't bear to look. The sounds gave a clear enough indication of the horrendous methods the man was using. In her delirious state she understood that Hans was saying nothing. She hoped and even prayed it would all stop. She was in considerable pain but nothing compared to Hans. Again, she passed out.

***

"Are you all right dear?" Finally, a dog walker had arrived and Natalie felt better much better.

"Yes, I think so but I'm lost. Can you explain to me how to return to this address please?" Natalie gave her the piece of paper where she hoped Max had finished his filming and they could return home.

"Yes, of course dear it's only around the corner and I live in the very same road."

The woman who was fairly ancient with hairs sprouting from all the wrong places took her out of the park, which led straight on to the road she had come from.

"Do you know the man who is painting his house?"

"Yes, my dear I live next door."

"It's sad about his wife dying?"

"Oh no, he isn't married. He's a teacher I believe."

She could see Max sitting in the car. He was a little perturbed when he saw her but tried not to show it.

"Here she is, my dear, your wife, is she? She got lost that's all. Were you worried about her?"

They both wanted her to be quiet and leave so they could reassure each other. When she finally did, she walked into the house next to Citizen X.

"Well there's a coincidence," Max was the first to say it though Natalie had thought the same.

"Have you finished darling, I so badly want to go home."

102

"Yes, for today though I will need one more visit I think, you don't have to come if you want to do some more sorting out."

"I'll decide later."

"Do you want to talk about it?" Max asked hesitantly.

"What? The fact I have lost my favourite wig?" She paused and lowered her voice as if ashamed, "Just more of the same, panic, nausea, fainting, flashbacks."

Max knew when to back off. "I got some good stuff, moving of furniture, stretching, push-ups."

"You're not serious about the push-ups?" She managed to smile

"No, and by the way I'm glad you lost the wig. I never liked it."

"You never said."

"Come on, let's go home, shall we?"

"Good idea and by the way he's lying about the wife."

"Oh yes, no ring, no photos of her and probably gay."

"No, more like a paedophile." Natalie looked away so he wouldn't see her smiling.

"Do you think so?" Max was always prepared to think the worst of human beings.

He tucked her up in bed and she slept all afternoon.

He took a phone call about 3.00 pm and felt the excitement as the caller described the job he required from the Versatile Detective Agency. This was much more like the work he wanted to be a part of. He took Natalie a cup of tea at 4.00 pm and suggested they go out for dinner as he had something to tell her.

"A new case?" She could read his mind now so just as well, Max, thought to himself that he never wanted to deceive her.

"Tell me now so I can become as excited as you appear to be." She moved closer to the edge of the bed where he was sitting and stroked his forearm.

"No, you can wait as our dinner will be with the man whose case we have taken on." He appeared to be in a hurry as instead of accepting her invitation to join him in bed he stood up. "You will have to wait my darling as I have to deliver this to our ever-anxious headmaster."

"That is finished with?"

"Yes, while you were sleeping I popped back and got some wonderful footage. I didn't even have to get out of the car as he was outside painting the windows perched on a ladder." Max chuckled.

"Will that be enough?"

"Will have to be. I'll be back for you at 6.30 pm precisely, can you be ready?" And he was already gone before she could answer.

Natalie rose quickly and ran a hot bath. She took her time as she had at least two hours and she had no intention of exerting herself with all the jobs that needing doing in the flat.

***

Rescue couldn't come quickly enough. It happened quietly in the night. A group of men dressed in black at least four with guns. They went straight to where Pablo had to be sleeping exhausted after his terrible actions that seemed to have lasted for hours. Amongst the four men was the old man from the airport. He must have been following them from the start, Natalie concluded. She was still on the floor where Pablo had left her bleeding and in considerable pain. He had tortured her mentally as well as physically, talking constantly about his relationship with Max, how he had grown up with him and had been his mother's lover. But this faded into nothing as she saw what he had done to Hans. He couldn't walk or talk. Pablo had broken his legs and removed his tongue. There was blood everywhere. To Natalie it appeared black. His blood had mingled with hers on the floor.

***

"Wake up darling, you said you'd be ready," he said this in a mild-mannered way as he knew only too well the signs. The therapists had all told him there would be relapses maybe forever or they might fade and even disappear in time.

"Are you sure you want to come, you don't have to. I can see you need to rest."

"Max, I think I should come. I should be with you. What happened to my wig?"

"It disappeared on your jaunt remember."

"Oh yes and you said you never liked it." Natalie smiled as she found enough energy to get out of bed.

"I remember I made the bath too hot that's what made me sleepy."

"You smell delicious so now get dressed please. Let me get you something to wear from the wardrobe." He pulled out her short black lace dress.

"This will do nicely."

"Where are we eating?"

"The Dorchester, the car is downstairs waiting, so get a move on love of my life."

It only ever took her a few minutes to get ready. She had no need for foundation, as her complexion was perfect. Even through puberty there were no spots, blackheads or eczema. The quality of her skin was often commented on and most women would not believe her when she said she didn't use face make-up. But she always used as much eye shadow and mascara she could to compensate for her deep-set eyes. He waited for her at the door. Every time she saw him, having not seen him for what might only have been for a few seconds, she delighted in his looks and felt a deep appreciation that he hadn't gone away when she refused to see him.

He had remained with her throughout the aftermath of Berlin. He had done more than that. He had cured her as much as was possible.

As she got into the black Mercedes she commented, "Our client must be very rich."

"Indeed, and very desperate."

"Why?"

"His daughter has absconded with a member of the IRA."

The journey from east to west London only took half an hour and as Natalie snuggled up to Max she remembered the day he came for her and said he would never allow her to be in danger again. She didn't believe him for a long time almost a year. She told him to go back to his wife and she never wanted to see him again. But his persistence and his sincerity brought her back from despair. He never gave up on Hans either and when she finally relented and went with him to see Hans she didn't want to send him away anymore. But it took eighteen months to agree to marry him. Hans was the best man. In his wheel chair he even danced at the wedding. His legs would never heal and he would never speak again but there were many ways to communicate.

She found herself in hospital wondering many things, how Pablo had gained the upper hand. Why had Hans been such a fool trusting him enough to get into the van? If they were being followed, why didn't help come earlier? Why did they accept the third note as being genuine? But what had occupied her thinking most of all in the following weeks as she healed up physically was how does a man become such a monster? She was told her injuries healed slowly for such a young woman. When Max arrived to take her back to England she refused to see him. She preferred to stay in a German hospital close to Hans and when she eventually returned to England and her flat she saw no one for at three months. Max called every day but she never let him in so he only called by once a week then once a month then not at all and that's when she realised she couldn't recover without him. She travelled back to the wig shop and left him a message with the same woman. No words were exchanged. This was her first excursion beyond north London and the beginning of what she called her second life. It could have been worse. She could be dead.

She went back to the coffee shop and felt better with a decent cup of coffee inside her and waited for Max. He arrived more quickly than she anticipated and she spoke first, "We were betrayed, weren't we? By our own side. What's that called?"

I didn't know and that's all Max said. And she believed him or chose to.

They began by holding hands. Then kissing but it took much longer to become lovers again. He took her to Florida, then Cuba. He still had connections that enabled him to freely travel there and basing themselves in Havana, Natalie began to recover emotionally. He showed her his childhood home and talked about everything she wanted to know. She had always been a good listener and the stories he told were therapy for them both. He told her the story of his mother and father, the story of his mother and other men, the story of his mother and Pablo. He told all of the stories on one particular day pacing the telling of the events slowly in harmony with their walking on that hot and humid day.

The chauffeur, if that's what he was asked politely, "All right if I drop you here only I can't get right in front of the door," he paused and carried on, "security and all that," he went on further. "IRA, you know."

"Yes, we know, we understand thanks, here's fine." Max helped Natalie out of the car.

"I'm fine Max."

"In those heels I'm not so sure but they do set your legs off particularly well."

At the large swing doors their coats were taken and they were shown to the table where a man looked anxious, too anxious to smile.

Guilty Consciences

Ned Soames was in his late fifties and ready to retire. He was overweight, a heavy drinker, a liar by occupation not choice who had suddenly found God or to be more precise Love through God. Again, not a choice that he would have made for himself – why should anyone want love at his age and the inevitable disappointed of its failure or loss. But his new partner had chosen God and had expected him to do the same. He had tried on that fateful day to reach the usual bench in the usual church to leave a message for a contact. It was a particularly valuable asset and he had always insisted on delivering the information himself. And there she was, his age though slimmer, much slimmer, dyed blonde hair in one of those beehives that reminded him of a time when he was slimmer and a great deal happier. She was in fact the new cleaner at the church and as she stood there with her mop he could see his future.

"Have you come to pray? Of course you have, over that side is clean."

"Thank you." As he knelt down and looked at the altar covered in candles and as the overpowering smell of incense reached him he felt the overpowering need to change. He almost forgot why he was there as he enjoyed watching her swaying body, cleaning the tiled floor. She was humming to herself. He couldn't decide whether he preferred the back view of her buttocks or the front view of her breasts.

He had done enough good and enough harm for one lifetime now he wanted some peace. He never told her, Yolanda, that he wasn't religious. Nor did he tell her what he had done as work. He never told Max, who refused the wedding invitation that he had given the millionaire Matthew Worthington the name of the Versatile Detective Agency. The service had continued to follow Max's movements from the day he resigned to the day he

108

returned home from his extended honeymoon. On Max and Natalie's return to Heathrow, Tom was there and having now succeeded into Max's job he was determined to keep an eye on him, in a helpful sense, of course.

"Want a lift home?" Tom smiled.

"If you insist, Tom, very kind of you."

"Oh, and I picked these up for you, your cards for your new Agency, very tasteful, the gold on black." Tom smiled again. This time Max didn't thank him.

"If it's OK, I kept one, just in case I need your services."

"Actually, Tom I think we'll make our own way home."

Natalie squeezed his hand to indicate she approved of his decision.

The millionaire had been an old Estonian friend who feared going to the police and so found himself in Ned's Soames' office.

"I can't help you, Matthew, this is a police matter." Ned was firm.

"But I can't bring them in."

"Why not? If it's a kidnapping you have no choice or pay the ransom, do you need a drink, and we can go out for lunch and sort this out," Soames said kindly.

"Don't you have a bottle in your drawer anymore?" Matthew appeared puzzled.

"No, Yolanda has persuaded me only to drink wine and only with a meal. She's happy with that. I would have given it up completely but she's Italian as you know and Europeans like to drink."

"I'm glad you've found some happiness, Ned, and like me you've been alone too long."

"Don't blame yourself Matthew, she was always a wild one…and I gather this was no kidnapping."

"No, but I think it may turn into that, although she went willingly, this chap will surely start asking for money."

"Are you sure he's in the IRA and not just Irish?" Again, Ned was being as gentle as he could but always felt Matthew had more money than sense.

"I don't know and as I haven't heard a word from her since she sent me a postcard from Belfast six weeks ago I have no way of knowing." He had started to cry.

"She's all I have now Ned."

Ned had not yet handed in his resignation and he had no idea why he hadn't. It was as if there was something he needed to do, one last thing though he was clueless as to what it might be. One thing he knew it wasn't going to involve him and the IRA.

"Here." Ned handed him a small card, "I can trust this man to do his best for you but don't ever divulge the fact I suggested it."

Matthew walked home clutching the card in his right hand. It had started to rain but he had stopped crying and felt a flicker of hope.

He spent that whole evening looking at the card and the next morning. Doubts appeared in his mind. Maybe he should go to the police and report her missing.

She had left a note stating she had fallen in love with an Irishmen and was going to live in Belfast with him. As soon as they were settled, she would contact him. Yes, she was sorry it all had to be a secret but he was an important man and she did so love him and they would all be together soon. She was such a child only seventeen with no idea of what she might be getting into. At 3.00 pm he picked up the phone and spoke to Max and arranged to meet that evening.

When he saw Max and Natalie, he saw a very attractive woman on the arm of an equally attractive man. They conveyed complete confidence but he was less impressed by that than the devotion they exuded towards each other as they were shown to his table and as Max pulled the chair out a little for her he was reminded of how he had loved doing the same for his own dear dead wife. They shook hands and Matthew brought the waiter across almost immediately with a small gesture. He was obviously a regular and he was accustomed to good service that was clear. He ordered champagne.

"I'm glad you could meet me so quickly and here is the note you requested to see for yourself."

"How did you find us Matthew?" Natalie believed in being bold from the start.

"In the local paper, I was attracted to the notion of versatility."

"Why do you think your daughter would welcome being found and brought home?" Max asked.

"I know her, she isn't like this, lacking in sense. She is my daughter who never brought friends home, never really socialised."

"You mean she's a perfect target for predatory males," Natalie interrupted Matthew who didn't seem to mind.

"I am in your hands entirely and must trust your judgments. If you think she is happy and I am wrong I will leave her alone."

"You said Maddie is seventeen and didn't socialise, why was that, Matthew?" Natalie thought it wise to probe.

"Because I am a rich man, Natalie, and have brought her up to be cautious. This man has groomed her without me knowing."

Max asked for the photograph of the man and studied it carefully as he sipped his champagne. The man looked familiar.

"Would you like to order? Please, anything you like."

Natalie realised she hadn't eaten much and the champagne had gone straight to her head. "Prawn cocktail and the gammon please."

"Oysters and steak, rare for me." Max smiled at Natalie.

"In that case, we will need a bottle of Chablis and a bottle of Malbec, I will also have the oysters and steak, medium rare." Matthew managed a smile.

"What is your fee? I would like us to establish what sort of a contract you require for my solicitor to have you check it before you embark on your…I don't know what to call it, your mission?"

Max smiled. "Call it what you like."

"What is your number one outcome?" Natalie asked the question.

"Without a doubt her safe return and for that you can name your price."

"A four-bedroom house somewhere nice like Hampstead." Natalie sipped her champagne.

"Accepted," Matthew answered quickly enough.

"And your number two outcome?" This time Max asked the question.

Matthew took a sip of champagne. "The absolute assurance alongside the evidence that she had gone willingly and is happy and prepared to prove it by inviting me to meet him."

"Is that still worth a four-bedroom house in Hampstead?" Natalie interjected.

"Yes." The first course arrived. Only Natalie could now speak as the oysters occupied their mouths fully but instead she only had one thought and that was what was the third option but she felt that should not be articulated. Keeping positive was their newly formed Detective Agency's only option at least for the time being.

Although she felt no inclination to say more she couldn't bear the silence either so she found herself talking about politics something no one wanted to talk about, especially in England.

"I expect she'll win by a huge majority, a pity the first woman prime minister has to be so unlikeable. They'll have to sort out her voice; no one will listen to anything unless she improves the tone and pitch and as for her delivery. I'm an ex-drama teacher so I notice these things. She also needs to improve her posture. Her walk on those heels will cause her great problems as she gets older and then there are the handbags."

"Do you have children?" Matthew avoided the politics.

"No." Max and Natalie spoke together. The red wine was brought to the table indicating the imminent arrival of the second courses.

"I wish we had had more children but it never happened and now the one I have has disappeared."

Thankfully the waiter arrived to clear and the wine was offered for tasting to the men of course. Maybe a female prime minister would be a good thing.

Her mind wondered, the champagne had done its work, flashes of pain mixed with a wild and angry face.

"Excuse me, I need to go to the bathroom."

Sitting on the red velvet chair, her head spinning in a beautiful cool wash room at The Dorchester.

***

"There is no excuse, he is a monster."

"No, Max, I need a better explanation."

"Yes, but I don't know how to start or give you an answer."

"Let me try then."

"At the beginning after you discovered his affair with your mother when you were so angry you got on the first flight out of Miami. The flight to London you remember where you were

112

recruited and sent to Cambridge where you spied on the spies. Then when you lied to your mother about forgiving them and asking him to join you in Cambridge and turned him and he promised to be truthful always and then you sent the woman who looked so like your mother but younger and you knew he would love her as he did your mother and then she revealed she was working for the KGB and if he loved her – really loved her he would come with her and cross to the East and he could be a double agent and sell secrets to both sides and live and love and then disappear."

"Was that how it went Max?"

***

She returned from the washroom. The lipstick was refreshed, the hair was massaged back into place and the skin had been given another chance to impress with eye make-up renewed and perfume reapplied. It was for Max, it was always for Max. She didn't enjoy the gammon with the slice of pineapple on top but she enjoyed the taste of the white Chablis and the obvious admiration of a sad lonely man whose wife had died and his daughter had gone missing. He had been handsome once, now bald wearing thick glasses that didn't suit his face hiding a pair of soft brown eyes. At least he was keeping trim unlike older men she met. Max could see she wanted to go, go home and find some pleasure in the flesh. She lit a cigarette and took no more interest in the conversation. She was polite enough to smile and say goodnight to Matthew but hastened to the car that would drive them home and back to her security. Her desire for Max became an embarrassment to the driver but Max knew what to do and how to manage the situation. He was aware of the driver watching but that would never bother him and Natalie never noticed on such occasions. He marvelled at her lack of inhibitions and only momentarily compared her in this respect to his ex-wife. She had prepared herself the possibility of sex on the way home. The chauffeur drew the curtain that would exclude him from the act but he could still hear and after the joy he heard crying and then softly spoken words of reassurance and then silence. He thought she possessed a serenity that he wanted to share. He fantasied about her and how one day if she ever became unhappy he would be there for her like some Prince Charming but she already had one. As they got out of the car she smiled at him and said, "Will you go back for Matthew?"

"Oh no he will stay at The Dorchester."

"What's your name?"

"Sam, miss, goodnight, lovely to meet you."

"Goodnight and thank you Sam. You drive so well and with such consideration."

"Don't forget to vote tomorrow." He laughed.

"And who should I vote for Sam?"

He shrugged his shoulders and drove away.

"Do you have to relate to every Tom, Dick and Harry?"

"Max, that man had the privilege of hearing us making love in his car and he dealt with it with great panache. He was almost a part of it."

"You know, Natalie, I sometimes think your sexuality is more male than mine."

"Is that a problem?"

"Only if you behave like the majority of men which does not include me."

They flung their clothes off and fell asleep in each other's arms.

Matthew Worthington spent the night with the call girl Louise. He always felt guilty and always thought about his wife both before and afterwards but she reminded him so much of his wife, the smile, the sense of humour, the way she slept on her back. Sometimes she would not stay and got annoyed when Matthew offered her extra money and once when he was drunk when he asked her to marry him she was furious.

"Don't be ridiculous, what would your daughter say?"

She did stay on this occasion because she knew about his daughter's disappearance and felt sorry for him but she was up and out as soon as she woke up refusing his offer of breakfast in bed. It was a once a week meeting but for Matthew it was all he had to look forward to until his daughter returned.

Both Max and Natalie had slept well but already Natalie found herself thinking about her new home the one where she could walk to Hampstead shops, followed by a walk on the Heath. But more than anything they could bring Hans home. He would have a granny style apartment kitted out for all his needs and she could see him every day and make sure the care was sufficient and he never felt lonely. He had never complained about the home, which was paid for by the service but she knew he was lonely and he always put up with her chattering whereas Max often switched off which Natalie found mildly irritating. Its only advantage was that it was by the sea and that gave her the excuse to travel to Brighton once a week and after seeing Hans she would walk on the beach and then visit as many jewellery shops she could in the Lanes. The small and often crowded cobbled streets would take her in her imagination into history, which had been one of her passions at school. Little shops where you had to lower your head to get in and wooden beams would dominate overhead always looking too large for the shop itself. But she was sometimes too tired to enjoy the experience. The doctors had warned her that her head wound might always be a problem. Hans would never recover but he didn't complain, not that he spoke another word but he wrote a journal and she would read it on her visits. In it so much was revealed to her about his life and his friendship with Max.

One diary extract was particularly moving and enlightening:

Max was like a father and brother to me. He protected me on our missions together as a father and played with me as a brother, football, cards, drinking, dancing. I knew when he wasn't coming with us, it was because Pablo had also been like a brother to him, more so as he had spent much of his childhood with him and his mother. It should have been obvious to Max that Pablo could not survive the demands of being a double agent but perhaps it was the order to shoot her that turned him into the monster he became. First to take away one love then another and expect him to carry on and be loyal. He must have hated Max at the end.

***

Max woke up and asked her what she was thinking.
"How are you going to find out who this man is?"
"Remember Tom, who used to work for me, he owes me."
"Are you going back to the office?"
"Yep, are you coming?"

"No, I'm getting this flat sorted."

"There's plenty of time for that." Max flicked the duvet over her to reveal his naked body. He walked towards the bathroom.

"No, there isn't." Natalie propped herself up. Max turned and smiled as she said, "Because we'll be moving to Hampstead soon."

"If you say so."

Max had let his dark hair grow long because he knew that she liked it that way. What he didn't know was that it reminded her of her father. A man she saw rarely because he worked two jobs, managed to buy a car, several in fact not to take the family out but to boost his standing with the neighbours because he was a Jew and at that time it appeared everyone was an anti-Semite. He had disappeared out of their lives on a rainy Friday afternoon saying he would be back later that evening but they never saw him again.

The day was long for both of them but more difficult for Max. On entering his old office building he had a strong desire to blow it up. If the IRA had known its whereabouts maybe they would save him the trouble. His anxiety increased as he approached the receptionist who smiled, having recognised him immediately.

"And who have you come to see?" Mandy almost sang out the question. She had always been there at reception and she had always been accommodating. She had slept with everyone in the office. He recalled he himself had spent one night with her many years ago. He didn't remember much except that it had been pleasant enough.

"Tom actually, is he about?"

She stopped smiling, "Yes but…" and she hesitated, "he's in your office."

"Don't look so concerned, Mandy. I know he has my job and I know the way."

The story had been put about that Max had been sacked as a result of the Berlin debacle. He was happy with that as they had offered him a very pleasing deal which he knew was to keep him quiet. It had been a calamity but a planned one. Natalie and Hans were human bait to draw Pablo out. He hadn't been a party to that particular part of the plan but he had had his suspicions all along. He wondered whether they had wanted Hans and Natalie back alive as they could have got there sooner. But for everyone's silence they were paid off handsomely.

"Hello Tom, I like what you've done to the office, may I sit down?"

"Yes, yes of course, how are you? How are they?"

"As you might expect." Max did not smile and pushed his hair back off his face.

"I want some information and it's urgent. Who is this man?"

Tom knew who it was as the man was not only familiar but the photograph he himself had given to Soames.

"Where did you get this?" Tom looked at it more closely just to make sure; yes, it had the same date in the same writing on the back.

"Don't worry yourself about that," Max said impatiently.

"What if I can't tell you?"

"You will tell me, otherwise I will tell your wife."

"That's blackmail."

"Indeed, and I will continue to blackmail you for as long as I need to."

"Why, I told you I didn't know the plan I was your assistant remember?"

"And a very well informed one too. Now who is he?"

"Sean McBride."

Secrets Revealed

Max arrived home carrying the photocopied file of the IRA activist known as Sean McBride. Tom had been very responsive to Max's request. There once was a strange kind of trust that existed between them based on mutual respect. Tom had married his long-term childhood sweetheart with enthusiasm and a belief that their love would last forever. She had as she put it, "saved herself for him and her wedding night." Tom was a patient man but his wedding night was a disaster and he hadn't been able to rise above the shame and humiliation ever since. His new wife was disappointed not about the sex but about the strong possibility she might not have children. She tried everything from red to black underwear, stockings, magazines, sex toys, and even a variety of wigs. Max commented to Tom that she was showing such initiative maybe she should apply to MI5. Tom didn't appreciate the joke and left the pub in tears. They didn't speak for at least two days and when Tom left work on the third day without saying goodbye Max followed him. Tom entered Soho and the pub that was well known for picking up a partner of the same sex. Max waited across the street until Tom came out with a young man probably under the legal age. Max wasn't surprised, it was probably as common in the service as it was everywhere else and marriage was always a cover but not an impenetrable one. Max bided his time before he revealed to Tom he knew. Max blackmailed people all the time but this was close enough to cause a little uneasiness and he would only use the information when absolutely necessary. It had now become necessary for Tom to comply as his and Natalie's future depended on it.

Natalie was out; it was late afternoon, about 5.00 pm Max looked at his watch and wondered where she might be but was overwhelmed by the changes that had taken place in the flat, it had been transformed. It looked like a show flat. Books were on shelves in order of height, records were neat on the shelf above their record player, and the tapes previously scattered around the place were now in alphabetical order above the cassette player. There were new rugs on the wooden floors in the bedroom and lounge. Where had they come from? The kitchen walls had hooks and utensils placed on them, the order of which was a mystery to Max, perhaps by shape or size of handle? He would try to remember to ask her: she would like that. He made himself a cup of real coffee; the only sort he would drink and then he sat down to read the file.

Natalie having finished with the flat was exhausted but on a high. She had found herself becoming obsessed with putting the final touches to the bathroom. Being unfamiliar with the area, she lived in and still cautious about getting lost, had caught a cab to Hampstead and found her way to the alley market, which stayed open till late on a Thursday. She bought a second-hand brass soap dish, a small fern plant and a glass perfume bottle with a pump spray. She bought a brass-framed mirror, not too large as the bathroom itself couldn't have been more than six feet by four. She found the pharmacy open and bought herself a large bottle of Parure by Guerlain and some tampons for when her periods arrived. She caught a cab home and as she rang the doorbell not wishing to hunt anymore in her bag. Max opened the door with a smile and said, "Have you voted?"

"Christ no."

"Well there's still time and the flat's looking very sellable."

"Yes, I thought so."

"Are they the final touches? Where shall I put them?"

"They're for the bathroom."

"Is there room in the bathroom for anything?"

On waking up that morning May 3rd neither of them felt the need to switch on the radio. It was obvious that Margaret Thatcher would be Prime Minister. Max and Natalie had been on their extended honeymoon throughout the so-called winter of discontent but they had read about it and listened to the BBC world service. In Cuba in particular they had engulfed themselves in another way of living. They rented a small beach hut on the north east of the island hoping to finally cast off the horrors of Berlin. It was in Cuba they shared their early life

119

experiences. The happy times Max shared with Pablo filling the void of an absent mother and a dead father. When his mother did return to their Cuban home two words came to his mind sex and secrets.

For Natalie it was the same only in her case she pined for her father who was away most of the time returning briefly to her alcoholic mother. Natalie was her mother's second attempt at motherhood. The first child a boy had died. They had been close for a long time but now Natalie found it hard to be with her mother.

***

Max tried reasoning with Pablo but he had fallen hard for the woman.

"She's betraying you Pablo."

"You introduced me to her."

"Only to take your mind off my mother."

"Well it worked, now leave us alone."

It was raining when he followed her. She went straight to the Stasi office and when she came out he followed her again. He knew she was meeting Pablo but he made sure she never got there.

"So he never forgave you for whatever happened to her?"

"I was genuinely trying to help him Natalie, he just seemed to lose his rationality. He became reckless and unpredictable but I told the service someone else would have to sort him out, there was too much history between us."

***

Born in 1947, Sean McBride was the youngest of seven children, brought up on a farm in Donegal quite close to the border near Lifford. All seemed fine until one day in the summer of 1969 his father disappeared according to his mother in the middle of the night. In fact, Sean's father according to MI5 was a senior member of the Provisional IRA and had not been kidnapped but had left to help organise the opposition in Belfast. The Battle of the Bogside as it became known was a three-day riot between the RUC and the Catholic residents of Bogside.

Eventually the British Army was deployed to restore order in Belfast where most of the rioting occurred. These events were seen as the beginning of 'The Troubles'.

The story was a familiar one to Max. Sean became an activist when a stray bullet that he attributed to the British Army killed his father but for Max in the chaos that was Ulster it could have been anyone. His role was quite an interesting one. He had been sent to New York to an uncle who had made a fortune building skyscrapers. He had presumably been fairly successful as he made several trips leaving from Cork and returning to Dublin. He became of interest to MI5 but always eluded arrest, as evidence was slim. As well as being charming he was very handsome 'irresistible to women' Max smiled and showed Natalie his out of focus photograph.

"Mmm yes, I could bed him tall, dark and handsome just like you," she kissed the top of his head, "and with the soft Irish accent as well…"

"Now look at Matthew's daughter's photo."

Natalie sat down next to Max who was in his dressing gown on their small sofa.

She knew what Max was implying but resisted giving an obvious answer.

"Supposing she's very funny or hugely intelligent or good in bed."

"Natalie, this isn't funny."

"What would you like me to say, he's trapped her in love to get her dad's money. Well why hasn't he demanded a ransom yet? Don't answer that, I know. It's not so much the money as the world she lives in, well used to live in." Natalie looked at Max.

"Correct he's after information connected to her father's world in order to cause havoc."

"You mean bombing a member of the establishment."

"Exactly," Max said with complete conviction.

"I'll go and do some research at the library." Natalie felt like getting out.

"Yes, a family tree and I'll go a see my contact at MI5."

"Give my love to Tom." Natalie got up and as he tried to pull her down all she said was: "I'm going to have a bath and listen to the news on the radio."

Max was struck by the fact that the new Prime Minister would never give in to terrorists. She had made that very clear during her campaign.

He met Tom in a rather shabby pub in Soho.

"How's the marriage." *A strange way of greeting anyone*, Max thought.

"You mean how's Natalie?" Max sat on a stool that looked like it could snap in two.

"She's up more than down at the moment. How's your marriage?"

"Bloody awful if you really want to know." Tom was on the whisky at midday these days and made no attempts to hide it.

Max had ordered himself a soda water. "Why don't you tell her, Tom, and save yourself a great deal of suffering."

"I'm not suffering. I'm doing what I want, when I want and I can now do it with her, well sometimes. She's not highly sexed so she's easy to please."

"How did you get to be so…" Tom interrupted him before he could finish his sentence.

"I had a great teacher who deceived his wife very successfully when he recruited the lovely Natalie and then went on to blackmail me." Tom was almost in tears. Luckily the pub had no customers other than them and it was so dark Max wondered if it was midnight rather than midday as the small artificial lamps were on.

"The blackmail would stop if you revealed your true self, I would have nothing on you and would leave you alone."

"Is that what this meeting is about? No, I thought not. You want more info on Sean McBride, don't you? Well I gave you a copy of the file and that should be enough, right?" He got up to buy another whisky.

Max felt sorry for him. Tom almost tripped up on his way back to the table. The carpet had holes and the surface of the carpet was uneven and stained.

"Next time we meet, I'll buy you a proper lunch."

"I don't want your lunches or your sympathy now what do you want?" Tom spat out the words.

"What's going on in Belfast?"

"Well not a lot after the carnage of the last few years the IRA are quiet and civil rights will happen sooner rather than later. Of course, a real settlement is rather far off as the new Prime Minister won't talk to them."

"So, what are they doing in this quiet period?"

Tom drew in his breath. "In my opinion they are saving up resources for a more serious and sustained attack so they will need to get arms which cost money more than they could get from extortion and it's more difficult for them to rob banks with the army there."

"Apart from money from taxi/cab services, would they kidnap anyone for money?"

"Don't see why not." Tom frowned. "But it's risky in terms of PR."

"Do they care about that?"

"Max if they want to be taken seriously they won't go down that route particularly if the family are part of the British establishment."

Max pondered on his next question, "Supposing there's a rogue element, young and disobedient, wanting to piss off the IRA leaders."

"It's more likely to be a power struggle between those who want to fight and those who want to talk."

"But if the British government won't talk."

Tom finished off Max's thought for him, "Then 'The Troubles' will start again and probably quite soon."

Max lightened the tone, "So you wouldn't recommend a holiday there?"

"You'll be all right for a few months but come winter. I'm getting another drink. Bye, Max."

Natalie had trouble finding a library locally so found a tube got on the Piccadilly line and went to Russell Square where she knew there was a library attached to The Institute of Education. She had been sent there on courses during her teaching time. She smiled at one particular time when she was on a course concerning the teaching or rather handling of Cypriot boys. There had been an influx into mainly Haringey schools after the crisis in Cyprus. She failed to understand the politics but understood only too well how different the male culture was or rather how more overtly sexist it was compared to English culture.

However, that wasn't the focus of the course, why would it be when even English boys and men were only just beginning to realise men and women were equal. They weren't yet behaving as if equality was desirable but they were at least acknowledging the debate and it would soon be the expectations of the educated females in Britain. Cypriot boys were several generations behind. When she refocused the course around the topic of sexism she was asked to leave it by the man who ran it. Instead of being disappointed she happily left and spent the rest of the day shopping. The next day no one showed any interest in what she had learnt and the new trendy cascading concept yet again failed to materialise. Instead she simply got the usual about how difficult her classes had been and that the cover work was unsuitable.

She liked the atmosphere in libraries. The library was tucked away in Ridgemount Street in an old office block. People seemed relaxed and content in their own company but she hadn't a clue where to start. The librarian sent her to the Who's Who section and she found the appropriate large marooned leather-bound book and she lifted it on to the nearest table. A young man looked up at her and helpfully moved his bag so she could use the table more freely. She opened the book and quickly found Matthew Worthington's page. He was a successful lawyer, industrialist and writer who had published a book on exotic birds, a book about the nature of friendship and a third book on the reason to have a monarchy. This attracted her attention and she found herself looking for the book called *Without a Monarchy* – a strange title for a book in favour of it. Natalie reminded herself of how she and Max had thankfully missed all the street parties celebrating the Queen's Accession to the throne. They had got away to the Caribbean as soon as she had physically recovered and Hans was able to smile again. He reassured her that he wanted her happiness more than his own because knowing she was happy helped him. He had promised to be well on their return. She grimaced as she thought about his lack of progress. She badly wanted him nearby and with the success of this mission she would get a house big enough for him and his own personal carer. She couldn't find the book and returned to Who's Who. She forced herself to concentrate but what she was looking for, a family tree wasn't there. It wasn't a particularly long entry but suddenly it jumped of the page. He lived in Ireland for two years—Ulster outside Belfast where he had several factories making kitchenware for the British Army. She was so excited she laughed out loud and smiled broadly at the young man. He took his glasses off and watched her as she returned the mighty tome to its shelf. She thought about searching again for his book on the monarchy but decided she would order it in and return another time. The librarian was a tiny woman who looked ridiculous as she emerged from behind a pile of books but she had a warm smile and sweetly said, "How may I help you?"

"Can you locate this book for me by tomorrow?"

"No need to, it's right here. Someone just brought it back. Do you have your card?"

She thought quickly, "Yes it's in my bag just over there but can I just flick through quickly to see if I really need to take it home."

"Of course, dear." Another sweet smile.

Natalie returned to the table. The young man watched her as she boldly put it in her bag and left the library.

Natalie found the tube station easily enough although it wasn't the one she had come out of. This one was Goodge Street on the Northern Line perhaps best known for its grubbiness and unreliability. Unfortunately, it only had a lift and Natalie couldn't enter a lift at the moment. Max assured her it was a temporary hitch and he liked using stairs himself, a good way of staying fit and lean he told her. So, she walked on to Euston and found she couldn't face the escalators. She would get a taxi and to hell with the cost. Max was home when she arrived. He saw from the window that she had taken a taxi and he hoped she would be all right. She flounced through the door, her eyes alive with excitement and he listened as she divulged her discovery.

"Very impressive my darling. Make us something to eat and I will scour the book for further insights."

He heard her open a bottle of wine and knew she would drink the whole bottle unless he helped her. He wanted to get to a time when an evening consisted of tea or coffee.

Max found reading the book rather tedious but the photographs were much more interesting. They seemed to suggest that Matthew was quite close to some members of the Royal Family. A further discussion with Matthew was essential before they headed off to Ireland. He would arrange that tomorrow. He just settled down to eating his chicken casserole made with a little too much garlic for his taste when the phone rang. It was his ex-wife.

"Got to go after I've eaten the teenager is causing ructions again."

"What now?" Natalie wanted to be with him this evening.

"Apparently she's run away! I won't be long."

She finished the bottle of wine and saw it was late. She'd already had her fill of Thatcher who had the nerve to quote Francis of Assisi as she entered Downing Street. She curled up on the small sofa waiting for Max. She thought about what he had said on their honeymoon.

***

By the time I had got to Cambridge they had caught my mother. She had slept with a CIA agent without knowing. One of her one-night stands but according to Pablo she couldn't resist him, a Steve McQueen look alike. He listened in like I used to as a kid. He was furious but it helped propel him into my arms and he left the next day. She was taken for interrogation and never left prison. It took me awhile to get him out of the states but the CIA were moving in on him at a rapid rate. Funnily enough he always claimed she never betrayed him but how else would they have known, yes, I think about her sometimes but once they finished with her they improved her conditions. She's allowed out for a walk once a week and I believe she now has a cell with a window. It was always Pablo I felt sorry for. Once the Stasi realised he was a double agent, they tortured him for months.

"Why did they let him go?"

"They thought he was finished and besides they kept a close eye on his movements. But he was quietly waiting for his revenge."

***

She shrieked when he came in creeping around the sofa.

"Sorry, I thought you'd be in bed. I had to drive round to find my rebellious daughter. She was at the bus station smoking with a gang of friends."

Natalie said nothing and went into the bathroom, cleaned her teeth and got into bed. When Max tried to caress her, she moved away.

"Why didn't he take his revenge on you?"

"Because you were there and I wasn't."

"But you could have been. You could have come instead of Hans."

"We've gone through this, Natalie. I was your handler and not an operative anymore. I wasn't allowed to go. That's the way it is in the service. Those are their rules."

Tough Decisions

Matthew Worthington had agreed to meet Soames at his club on the same evening that he had agreed to meet Max. It was a calculated move on his part to clarify for himself what was going on now and what would happen in the future. Matthew had been suffering the deep anxiety of not knowing what was happening to his daughter Maddie and the agony of his own inaction. He hoped this meeting was going to make him feel more in control.

Soames was his usual punctual self and sat down opposite Matthew at 7.00 pm precisely. They had always sat in the same place in the same dark red leather chairs by the same open fire under an oil painting of King Charles the first. It always amused them that no one would use these chairs that they were always empty as if the two had booked this spot every evening at the club. It's true there was a time when they had reserved it every evening. They had both been acutely lonely, no wives to go home to. The overweight chief of MI5's European section and the lonely once handsome industrialist would come to console themselves in the very same chairs, ordering the same supper and conversing about better times. But then Soames had met Yolanda and she wouldn't allow him to go anywhere where women were not welcome. At first, he had found this a strange notion but Soames was as sick of his club as he was of his job so this rare and nostalgic visit made a nice change. Yolanda had gone to a special church service that evening so it all fitted in quite well. The club was virtually empty probably the Tory members celebrating Thatcher's triumph elsewhere so they could be noisy and obnoxious. It was an unusually warm evening and the fire hadn't been lit. There were two other men in the far corner of the small dark room talking quietly as these two intended to do. Already on his third whisky, Matthew was getting emotional. He leaned forward and revealed that he had invited Max to join them.

"Time to reconcile, don't you think?" Matthew said with the confidence provided by the whisky.

Soames smiled. "I'm not the problem and I'm hoping to retire soon maybe at the end of the year. I will face Max anytime but I've already told you I didn't want him to know I was involved in any way, however peripherally."

Matthew slumped back in the chair. "Don't you think he's worked it out."

"Look, Matthew, if he thinks MI5 is involved, he'll probably back out."

"He can't, he's signed a contract and besides he needs you. He uses Tom as a source all the time, here he comes." Mildly irritated by this comment Soames decided to stay.

Max could have walked out but asked himself what would he gain? He would look foolish and appear immature besides he would miss out on some rather good whisky.

"Grab a chair, Max I'm too pissed to move and Soames here is not sure he's staying." There was an awkward silence but then Ned said, "I'll stay and finish my drink but I know you will want to talk privately."

Max pulled up a stool and played along. "Indeed I have a lot of questions to ask Matthew but you may be able to help me as well."

"I can't, and you know that." Soames shifted himself forward as if to leave.

"But you wanted me on this job, didn't you? Why so shy about it? Why didn't you just ask?" Max moved the stool closer to them.

"Let's get some more whisky and relax a little before you two upset each other." Matthew signalled and smiled at the waiter. "I asked both of you here together to help me get my daughter back."

Soames who had leaned forward as if to leave slowly leaned back in the chair, which squeaked as if it approved. "All right, I will stay for another drink. But this is how it will be. I will nod if you are on the right track." Matthew found this suggestion rather funny and proposed a toast: "To the return of my daughter."

Soames proposed another toast, which shocked them both

"To the demise of Margaret Thatcher!"

"That's a bit risky in here." Matthew had stopped laughing.

"It's the only hope for peace in Ireland," Soames spoke in a serious tone.

Natalie had intended to go to the library to return the book she had acquired without consent. She had seriously considered not returning the book as she would have to figure a way of disguising her deceit in the first instant and her second consideration was she dreaded another attempt using the tube. She could think of a number of things she would rather do, shopping for their trip to Belfast being one of them. She solved the problem of travel in the usual way and went by minicab. In the mini-cab she had forced herself to acknowledge that her real motivation was the fact she wanted to show the young man that she was an honest person. There was no guarantee he would be there but she somehow felt he would. There he was, same table covered entirely by his bag. She took time to look at him closely. He was handsome with a boyish face, and the kind of long hair that looked like it, despite its length had been well cut. He looked clean wearing flared blue jeans and a loose black woollen jumper. She had no idea why she found him interesting but she walked straight up to the table he was sitting at and without thinking slammed the book down.

"That's a bit aggressive, isn't it?" but the young man was smiling at her. Natalie didn't speak not because she didn't want to but she couldn't think of anything to say.

He continued talking as he moved his bag, "My name's Craig, you are welcome to sit here again."

"I'm not staying, I don't like libraries." Natalie didn't move.

"And you don't like taking the tube either?"

Natalie remained still taking in the full implication of this question or rather statement.

"Especially at this hour, so I had better hurry."

"I can escort you if you like."

"I don't live alone."

"That's OK, I don't have to come to your door."

"You can if you want, he's out for the evening."

"Well let's get going." Craig looked down at the book. "Leave it, the librarian will think nothing of it, people do it all the time."

Travelling with Craig on the tube home was a strange but reassuring experience.

They didn't speak much only about the different stations and how the tube lines interacted. Natalie wondered if this was some kind of code or whether he was just trying to make her feel comfortable using the underground. Either way she found herself trusting this young man probably younger than her and when they got to her flat she almost invited him in, a complete stranger. He noticed the light under the door before she did. He was already walking back down the stairs when he turned and smiled and whispered

"Come and see me again, you know where to find me." Then he blew her a kiss. She wasn't shocked, as it seemed the most natural thing in the world.

She had her keys out ready but Max must have heard her because he opened the door and smiled.

"You look happy." He kissed her at first affectionately then as he used his tongue the excitement rose in both of them. They hadn't made love for a week.

"I'm not sure I want to go with you to Belfast," Natalie spoke in the darkness. "I'm not sure I'm ready for this. I can't even handle the London Transport system let alone the chaos of Belfast."

"I'm not leaving you behind and I think you are ready," Max spoke with conviction.

"Your faith in me is impressive but I don't want to leave Hans."

"Natalie we are doing this for Hans, and I will need you. I can't do this without a partner. You are my cover story. It's all worked out." Max moved closer to her and stroked her back. She switched the bedside table lamp on.

"Tell me then."

The next day Craig was sitting in Soames' office feeling pleased with himself. It was early, some of the cleaners were still there.

"Well give me any relevant details." Soames had indigestion and wasn't in a patient mood. He had stayed drinking at the club and found himself indulging in a late heavy supper consisting of rare succulent roast beef and all the trimmings. Yolanda had flatly refused to cook him any breakfast not that he wanted anything to eat and banned him from the club again.

"Darling it was a one off to comfort an old friend who needed my advice."

"Next time he comes here and you give your advice, I also help, yes?"

"Okay darling," Soames agreed knowing this could would never happen.

"Well?" Soames chewed and swallowed a couple of Rennies.

"She's still vulnerable, I would say."

"Would you like to expand on that, please." Soames was polite but showed his agitation through his voice.

"Well she can't handle noise, small spaces or crowds."

"Could she be persuaded to have an affair? An affair with you?" Soames had raised his voice. He had always believed Craig unsuitable for work in the field. He was an intellectual or was he just plain wishy-washy? Soames couldn't decide. His appearance seemed somehow to project weakness not strength.

"It's hard to say, I mean she's totally into him. I heard them through the door as I was leaving."

"Describe it." Soames always enjoyed the salacious part of the job.

"Well I could hear the moaning, the hasty undressing and you know, they didn't even make it to the bedroom."

"Were you seen?"

"No, of course not. You know sir I don't think she's going to go for me, I'm so much younger and probably not that good at sex."

"Well get some experience, we have to break up this unholy alliance."

"May I ask why, sir?"

"No, now go and meet up with her again and maybe she'd like a change, someone who fumbles around a bit, maybe she would find that gives her confidence." Soames was finding it difficult to cope with his wind and dismissed Craig with a wave of his hand.

Soames started to feel nauseous and wondered whether the food at the club had poisoned him. Full of self-loathing and a determination not to share this with his wife, Soames recalled his last visit to Max's still beautiful mother Rebecca. His promise to her as her ex-handler and only confidante was made rather hastily and of course out of selfishness, a desire to retire with something to impress those bustards that believed he had achieved very little in his role.

Her words surprised him. Max should stay with his family. His children need their father. This Natalie is too young and not even beautiful. His wife is – I knew her you know. I picked her before he did.

"I gave you Pablo."

"And I gave you a window in your cell. Next, you'll be asking for a sea view."

"Stop rambling and tell me what you can give me. I get the point. I will separate them if you make it worth my while."

"I will give you the name of Russia's spy deep within MI6."

The phone rang early but they decided not to answer it. An hour later it rang again and it was Max's ex-wife. Natalie leaned in towards Max and handed him the receiver. She played with the cord of the phone the whole time he was on the phone. This seemed to irritate him.

"She's run away again." Max grimaced.

Natalie leaned back and sighed, "For how long this time at least two hours? Her tone was sarcastic."

Max never liked her sarcasm and sent her a look of disdain and left the bedroom. Natalie followed him and suddenly felt brave enough to call him a hypocrite.

"You never cared before your divorce and me, so why now?"

"She's my daughter, she's up to god knows what and she hates her mother." Max was more emotional than she had seen him for some time. Natalie backed off and went into the kitchen to make some coffee. Max followed her and said, "The last time she did this and I took her back, we had a long discussion and she expressed her wish to live with me. I know we don't have the room yet but I promised her when we had the room she could. I should have mentioned it before. I'm sorry."

Natalie sat down at the small kitchen table and sipped her coffee. At this moment many thoughts entered her head but she thought it better to keep them to herself until she had decided on what she felt.

"You'd better go then, I'll see you later."

"What are you going to do today?"

"I think I'll go back to the library to do some more research."

Craig was astonished to see Natalie in the library at such an early hour,

"Had a row with your boyfriend?" He found himself blushing.

"As a matter of fact, I have so I've come here to find some kind of distraction."

"I could suggest a number of good books." Craig put his glasses back on then took them off again.

"No, I was thinking maybe a film or a play?" Natalie was starting to feel silly. This flirting was never in her nature.

"It's OK, Craig, I've changed my mind and I think I'll just go for a walk." She left the library and got a cab to King's Cross and a train to Brighton. Hans would make her feel better.

The carer who was from an eastern European country had never smiled before but as Natalie got out of a mini cab the woman came to greet her at the top of the steps. Her smile was a nervous one

"I saw it was you, Natalie. Thank you for coming so quickly." Natalie froze.

"You got the message, that's why you're here, yes?"

"I didn't get any message."

"But I spoke to Max this morning."

She didn't have time to take in Max's forgetfulness.

"What's the matter?"

"Hans is very weak."

"He's always weak, what are you saying?"

"He's dying Natalie."

Natalie ran quickly up the steps through the large wooden doors and along a winding corridor at the end of which was his room. The attending nurse said he was in a coma, after he had taken an overdose. The nurse explained how he had been saving up his painkillers and sleeping pills and then last night he took them all.

"Can he hear me?" Natalie asked quietly

"I doubt it. I'll leave you with him. Ring the buzzer if you need me."

Natalie held his hand and spoke to him,

"Remember when we first met. If I hadn't already been in love with Max I would have fallen for you but then you preferred men. I always knew."

She picked up his journal and she thought she saw him smile. She read the latest entry.

I know you read this my dearest friend and so I want you to know I never regret meeting you though I do regret not listening to you that terrible day. I know how you have suffered and I want to make it right by leaving you to move on with your life with Max and yes without me. I know you want me with you in that big house but it's over for me and you are the only one who can grasp that so you must let me go.

Take the journal with you when you leave. It was written for you so that we can still converse. You will know everything about me. Please follow the instruction on the piece of paper and destroy it before you leave me lying comfortably in my bed. Close my eyes.

There was a separate piece of paper, folded at the front of the journal, his own handwriting giving her a clear message and ensuring her actions would have no repercussions, she checked the door was closed and sat on the chair beside the bed. His eyes were already closed. She sat with him and wondered why he had never recovered to a more active state. He had been so strong at the training camp. But he had a deep sadness and he now looked contented. She kissed his forehead after she placed the pillow back under his head. She sat there for a long time; she thought that would look less suspicious. She wanted to avoid any conversations with staff. She wanted to tell Max what she had done. She would call him.

Clutching Hans' journal, Natalie walked out of the building straight into Craig, almost knocking him over. Her eyes wild and full of tears he was the last person she expected to see.

"Are you following me?" She screamed at him but before he could finish.

"Of course you are. What the fuck do you want?"

Craig managed to blabber a few words but she didn't hear. She ran out to the street into the phone box opposite to call Max but realising that was pointless as he might still be searching for his daughter. She came out of the phone box.

"Let me help you, Natalie. I'm not intending to harm you."

Natalie had learnt not to trust anyone except Max.

"Get me back to London. I'm in a hurry."

"Of course."

She sat next to him as he drove her back to London. She allowed him to take her to a hotel just for a drink he said. She felt incredibly tired not the sort that made you sleep but did make you weary, too weary to fight. He was a nice young man. Could he take her mind of things? Things she could never share not even with Max.

Mothers and Daughters

Max was striding round the lounge of Matthew Worthington's large rather gloomy house in Hampstead with the picture of a young girl gagged and tied up kneeling on the floor of what could have been a barn. There was straw but that didn't mean anything. The picture was dark and out of focus.

"How can you be sure it's her?"

"It came to my house in this envelope."

"Nothing else?"

"What do you mean?"

"A ransom note?"

"No. Are you all right, Max?"

"Not really as a matter of fact we appear to be in the same situation."

Matthew tilted his head and said, "Your daughter, has she been kidnapped?"

"Disappeared. Do you mind if I have a drink?"

"It's only 10.30 am."

"I know, but it will help me think." Max watched him pour a whisky from a half full cut glass decanter. He didn't tell him that Natalie was also missing. Three missing women and he hadn't a clue what to do about any of them.

**

The photos Craig had put on his desk didn't as much annoy as confuse Soames.

"Are these your buttocks or hers?" Before Craig could answer, Soames had picked up another photo. "Is this a position from the Kama Sutra?"

"The what, sir?"

"What's this, her hair's blonde not dark?"

137

"She wore a wig sir, she insisted."

"I'm not sure this will convince Rebecca."

"Who, sir?"

"Max's mother."

"Sorry sir but the technology could benefit from an upgrade."

"It's second hand from MI6." Soames paused.

"Tell you what, fax them over maybe her eyes are not as sharp as they once were and then come back and give me the details."

"Of what, sir?"

Soames didn't bother to answer just a withering look, which would be lost on Craig.

***

Natalie woke up alone in a large double bedroom. She was lying naked in an oversized double bed with possibly black silk sheets. The whole room seemed to be covered in dark wooden panels. There was a light on in the en-suite bathroom set opposite the window. The ceiling to floor curtains were dark, maybe maroon colour maybe velvet, heavy like her body. She managed to get to the toilet just in time before she wet herself. The floor was thankfully bright, with white marble tiles. The sunken bath looked inviting surrounded as it was by dark green marble tiles and fitted with brass taps so bright that they made her eyes hurt. She had a thumping headache and her head felt incredibly hot. When she looked in the mirror she permitted herself to shriek at her appearance. Her blackened eyes from the mascara stared out at her reflection and the wig was now only half on her head. She pulled the wig off violently and brought some of her own hair with it. She sat back down on the toilet and clearly remembered the last time she felt like this. She remembered the small hot interrogation hut better than she recalled the past few hours. A drink at the bar followed by a suggestion to go upstairs to a bedroom. She couldn't remember much else and wondered what had enticed her to go with this young rather awkward man whom she had come to trust and was fond of but not particularly attracted to.

Max went home. He couldn't think of any other option other than to sit and wait for Natalie to return. Hans' death had been reported to him almost twenty-four hours ago. A young man had picked up Natalie, according to the carers, in his twenties, they thought. They believed he was a mini-cab driver taking her to the station. She always took a mini cab to the station but he knew that.

Christ, he said to himself, what was she up to? What was Sean McBride up to sending a photo without any demands? What was Alex, his daughter up to? Running away and not phoning him to collect her and rescue her from her mother?

The door opened and Natalie walked in. She was remarkably calm. He could see she had been through an ordeal. But she remained calm as she spoke about how Hans had finally died and the stranger Craig.

"Can you remember anything after you arrived in the bedroom?" Max asked determined not to show how anxious he was.

"Yes, he made me a cocktail from the mini bar, we chatted and the next thing I remember was waking up, phoning a cab to come home."

"Did you realise you were being set-up?"

"Not at first I thought he was just interested in me but after the first time he followed me and then brought me back here and then he was at the care home I decided to go along with it whatever it is. I was testing myself. I've been such a burden not just on you but myself. I wanted to prove something but I guess I'm not ready yet."

"You'll be fine and there's one person I know will know what's going on. Will you be OK if I go out?"

"Yes, of course with this concoction of drugs inside me I'll just go to bed and sleep."

Max sat opposite Soames. "You wouldn't believe the number of visitors I've had today already. But at least I can get the whisky out with you, Max." Soames looked pleased with himself and Max knew he'd come to the right place.

"Do I have to ask what you are playing at or will you enlighten me?" Max spoke through gritted teeth.

"I take it she's alright?"

"Of course she is but I don't take too kindly to my wife being kidnapped, drugged and photographed doing all sorts of sordid things."

"Just photos, I can assure you, I don't think the chap is capable even when it's offered on a plate." Soames refilled Max's glass.

"But who for?"

"Come on, Max, can't you guess?" Soames smiled

"Christ Soames, don't tell me she's after a sea view."

"Do you know, that's exactly what I said?" They both laughed. Soames became serious and looked Max straight in the eye. "Max, I may need further help from you regarding this matter."

"I no longer work for you."

"If you help me get the information I need from Rebecca before I retire, I will help find your daughter and help you in Belfast."

Max had to admit to himself he hadn't quite anticipated this. He gave Soames his empty glass.

"What's your proposal?"

Max went straight home to check on Natalie. She woke up and called him into the bedroom. As he shared the plan with her he could hardly believe he had gone along with it.

"He needs me to convince her I have gone back to my family – the photos of your betrayal will just whet her appetite that's if she finds them at all convincing."

"You saw them?"

"Yes, and I met the bloke, what's his name Craig?"

"And this is in order to achieve what exactly?" There was anger in her voice.

"Soames gets the name of a double-agent at the heart of MI6 as a retirement present from my mother."

"And what do you get?"

"They will find Alex and help us in Belfast. We get our nice big house paid for by MI5 and live happily ever after." Max kissed her gently on the lips.

"Without Hans."

"Try not to be so sad. He wanted it this way."

"I know. Believe me I know. Do you mind if I go back to sleep?"

"Goodnight, my darling and thank you for being with me."

Max had had another phone call from Matthew Worthington and Max could hear the panic in his voice. Funny that, Max, reflected it's all in the voice, over the phone that is. He arrived within thirty minutes and sat where he had sat before with a glass of malt whisky waiting for him on the coffee table. He handed Max a brown envelope in which there were photographs but not of his daughter this time.

"Who is this?" Max was confused momentarily.

"It's a friend well he was a friend but I haven't seen him for some time. He is minor royalty, very minor. Why do you suppose this Sean McBride has sent me this?"

"Maybe he's a target for the IRA, maybe you are required to help them in some way. And there's nothing else?" Max needed more to go on.

"Yes, a short letter from Maddie, saying everything's fine."

"So, the previous photo, just a sex game eh?"

"Please don't joke Max."

"Yes, sorry Matthew."

"Have you found your daughter yet?" Matthew sounded sincere.

"No. Let me take this photo and see if I can find out where it was taken."

"It would have been taken in Ireland, that's where he lives." Matthew hoped he was being helpful.

"Good so they're following him maybe we can track down where the photo was taken."

"Oh, I know that's Belfast, the posh bit. I still have his address somewhere. Let me go and get it."

Max put the slow drip, drip of information from Matthew down to the stress of his daughter's abduction otherwise he might have strangled him.

Max called Soames as soon as he got home. Natalie was in the bath, happy and humming, he couldn't begin to fathom why. Yolanda answered and said in her heavy Italian accent that he was in the bath but would call him as soon as he was dry. He preferred a shower himself, must be his Cuban/American childhood. He waited no longer than five minutes.

"Hello Max, any news?"

"Yes, Matthew has located an area in Belfast where the possible target might be living."

"You mean the Royal bod?"

"Yes, Matthew says he's pretty minor doesn't even get invited to the garden parties."

"Soames sniffed, still might upset the royal household, if only to scare them. By the way, we found your daughter."

"What? Why didn't you tell me straightaway?"

"Because I'm telling you now. In fact, I've got my chap picking her up and bringing her to you right this minute so you can thank me."

"Thanks!" Max was filled with emotion, relief but he hadn't prepared Natalie.

"I'd better ring my wife, I mean ex-wife and tell her the good news. Where was she?"

"Now that you do not want to know and don't badger either." Soames hung up.

He went into the bathroom, she was still enfolded by bubbles and there was no sign of her body apart from her head.

"Hello darling, good news?"

"Yes, they found Alex, she's coming straight here. Is that all right?"

"Yes of course. Why don't I get out of the bath and make us something to eat or should we eat out or maybe you should go together and talk. I can stay in and watch *'The Sweeney'* or just read and relax."

"I tell you what, I will take her out with her mother as the three of us will need to sort something out. I'll meet her downstairs and see you later. Is that OK? I mean you've had such an awful time I should be with you."

"Max, go and don't worry I'll be fine." And she meant it. Something had happened and she felt it. She felt different since she had ended it for Hans. She had been tied into a nightmare and he was an integral part of it and it couldn't be put aside not while he was still there, visible and in pain. And while he was in pain she had to be. It was so simple. He had seen it and he had asked her to end it for both of them.

The meeting was tricky to put it mildly. He hadn't chosen a particularly good restaurant called Jimmy's in Soho. His wife disapproved of his choice and the area it was in but at least it had a range of cuisine, fairly unusual even in London.

"OK, don't eat but I'm sure Alex is hungry." Max asked for a menu. The place was warm, cosy and welcoming just what was needed on such an occasion.

He thought he would just dive in and start the decision-making process.

"This is the situation; our daughter wants to live with me not you. I don't have the room but I will have very soon and Natalie and I will take her when the time comes."

Alex spoke quietly and without any emotion in her voice, "OK, Dad."

"I'm not happy with that arrangement, Max. I don't trust you to prevent this happening again."

The waiter returned thankfully with the menus giving him a moment to think.

His wife Alice spoke quietly but firmly.

"She stays with me until she is eighteen, then she can do what she likes. I'm leaving now as I am not hungry, you can drop Alex home after your meal and chat."

"Was she always such a cold fish, Dad, is that why you left us?"

"I didn't leave you Alex."

"Yes, you did, you left all of us. We missed you so badly, Dad. She couldn't cope you know."

Christ, thought Max, *she's more mature than I gave her credit for.*

"Promise you won't disappear again."

Alex smiled for the first time that evening. "No, it's not all it's cracked up to be."

"What isn't?" Max asked anxiously.

"Drugs, sex and rock 'n' roll." She looked down at the menu. Max had always hated that expression.

"I think I'll have the Hot Pot."

Natalie fully expected Max to return home with Alex but he was alone.

"How did it go?"

"Badly, I think. But she's back home and says she won't disappear again."

"Well, that's a result." He didn't answer.

"Are you coming to bed?" Natalie called from the bedroom.

"No, not yet, I have some work to do."

143

The truth was he had some thinking to do about Alex. On the way back from Jimmy's to Finchley they had to stop twice to enable Alex to be sick.

"Sorry, Dad wasted the meal."

When she got back in after the second bout of vomiting he didn't drive but asked her to tell him what she had been doing for the past two days.

"I told you," she said with an uncharacteristic defiance in her voice.

"I am not taking you anywhere until you tell me the truth." Max had noticed how bad she smelled and it wasn't just vomit.

"I think it would be better if you asked the questions and I will answer."

"Truthfully?"

"If you can handle it."

This made Max furious but he contained his fury knowing what that would lead to.

"Where have you been sleeping?"

"The first night I slept under a bridge near Kings Cross, a woman said I could share her spot. I didn't sleep so she gave me some of her whisky to warm me up and then I got a couple of hours."

"Did anyone offer you drugs?"

"Yes, the next day."

"Did you have sex with anyone?" There was a silence. "Answer me!"

"Yes."

"Who with and where?"

"He was older, maybe your age, he thought I was a prostitute because he paid me but he took to a room in a hotel that was quite close and when he left he told me I could sleep there until morning." Max let his head rest on the steering wheel.

"Do you want me to go on?" Alex asked him with great hesitation in her voice.

"Yes."

"Back on the street with Moira, the woman who helped me on the first night, said I could work with her and pay for the drugs that way. She told me nothing was for free on the streets. I didn't know what to do. The man, that man, he wasn't a freak or

144

anything but I could see from the state of the other girls that I had been lucky."

"Did he use anything?"

"What do you mean?"

"A condom."

"No, he said he preferred it without."

"I bet he did," Max muttered under his breath.

"I would have come home eventually, I just needed…" Max didn't want to hear anymore.

"Tomorrow I will take you to a clinic to check you haven't picked up anything. I will pick you up early and suggest when you get home go straight to the bathroom and have a long hot bath and don't tell your mother anything; if you do, change the story considerably."

"Dad, are you angry with me?"

"No, just with the world that I can't protect you from."

Before he started the engine, he looked at her. She was beautiful with big blue eyes just like her mother's. Long dark hair just like himself that was tangled and dirty but that was easily rectified. It was the inside damage that may never be repaired.

He watched her go into the house and he saw his other two children Peter and Sophia waving at him from the window. For a split second he thought, *If only I hadn't met,* but he stopped before he thought of her. Instead he drove home listening to the music on the radio as loud as the volume would go. Pity it was Abba's 'Dancing Queen' still at number one.

He went to bed mentally exhausted and was relieved Natalie had fallen asleep. This was his fault and his burden to bear. He would tell her in the morning of his plans to visit his mother. Soames had booked the flight and wanted to brief him early the next morning but for once he would put his family first.

"You know relations between mothers and daughters are always difficult. I think that once you accept them for what they are you can still love them."

"Thanks, Natalie. I appreciate your advice but my priority is to ensure she hasn't picked up some sexually transmitted disease, so I can't really ponder on the finer points of relationships between mothers and daughters right now. If Soames rings, tell him I will be in as soon as I can."

"Do you want me to come with you?"

"I don't think you need to be exposed to the down and outs of London."

"I mean to see your mother."

Max stopped in his tracks. "Given the purpose of the visit is to convince her I no longer have anything to do with you, that wouldn't be a good idea."

"I don't mean go and see her just be around if you need me. OK, stupid idea! Are you sure you will convince her?"

"No, my lying skills have degenerated since I met you but I have to try."

Max kissed her and left.

Natalie went back to bed with Hans' journal. She hadn't looked at it since that day.

She made herself open it but as she looked at the pages her thoughts wandered. Her mother came to mind. She had been a strong woman, a kind woman capable of many things but poorly educated and a huge propensity for self-pity and that had to be her downfall. The drinking was social at first and clearly gave her the confidence to cope with the many strangers that walked in and out of the house. The lack of a male presence in the house would draw them closer together and when he returned from his long trips abroad they would separate for the short time her mother would try to create a marriage. They were a handsome couple, he was dark and tall, and she was fair and petite.

She would hear their lovemaking, her bedroom too close to ignore it. She never felt compelled to listen at the door the way Max did as his mother made love to strangers. That had always made her smile the idea of Max listening at the door and being told off by Pablo who ended up his mother's lover.

And then her father was gone after only a few days and the house would return to its normal rhythms. They would become close again and she would drink again keeping it mainly to the evenings but then starting at lunch, then breakfast, then sleeping it off then starting again, then Dad would return, then it stopped and so on.

Natalie got out of bed, had a bath then went out. She got on the tube, off the tube, changed lines, several times and got the tube home. She picked up the journal and at that moment Max returned

"Well, is she OK?" Natalie asked

"Results won't be back for a week but I'm optimistic, she says she only had sex the once." Natalie decided to ignore the remark.

"Did she explain why she left this time?"

"No, but I had an insight, history repeating itself, she reacts to overwhelming situations the way I used to – just leave, only I never went back." Until now the atmosphere was heavy between them, neither was optimistic about the past and it was creeping up on them in unexpected twists and turns.

"When are you off?" Natalie deliberately avoided further discussion.

"The day after tomorrow, you can come if you like, you could stay in Miami, south beach is lovely, and Max sounded cheerful."

"No darling. I'll be fine."

"Of course you will. You look pretty fine to me."

Mothers and Sons

The flight to Cuba was long and Max anticipated about ten hours of discomfort, bad food and that's before you even landed. He recalled that his mother enjoyed taking them out to restaurants but even she with all her acquaintances could never find a place to eat where the food was good enough and by all accounts from Soames under the communists it deteriorated even further. His disparaging remarks about the communes that promised fresh and affordable food throughout the land had failed and he lost interest in the conversation when Max retorted that there was now free education and healthcare for everyone. Soames was old school and the fight against communism and its defeat is was what he lived for and now the naming of the last British spy would be his retirement accolade to prove he had not wasted his years in the service. Soames would retire to Italy and he assured Max he would be most welcome with whichever wife he chose to bring. In answer to his question about going to Havana rather than to Miami first, Soames had muttered something about the CIA being involved with the visit but they knew nothing about why he was going other than a sentimental visit to his mother who was very ill.

He drank enough whisky to get him some sleep, he reckoned about three hours. At least he was booked into a decent hotel where he could recuperate from the flight before his visit to his mother. Havana was already warm in May and little had changed in Max's mind under Castro. The square was there, the clubs, the bars, the music. Every five minutes a different band, a different set of instruments, but always the same rhythms, and the salsa sound dominated. It was an energetic but sensual dance. The glory of it was you could dance with any partner: a lover, a mother, a daughter as it exuded passion, warmth and joy, emotion to suit any partner. So with surprising enthusiasm Max after a quick shower without unpacking he headed down to the bar for a Mojito and after a few cocktails he was dancing. The age of the woman had no relevance. They were all great dancers and they were there only to dance. Finally, he made contact with the CIA agent who would escort him to see his mother probably the next day. She wasn't dancing only staring at him from the bar, long blonde hair, dyed of course, a figure that indicated she wasn't eating the local cuisine and why would she? He walked towards her and ordered a whisky

"Would you like a drink?"

"Sure, why not, rum and coke and as much ice as you can extract from this bartender. My name is Katya. Nice to meet you Max."

"That's not an American name."

"No, my mother was Russian, spying for the Americans." She laughed rather nervously, he thought.

"And my mother was English spying for the Russians."

"And you?" Katya gave him the seductive eye contact combined with a flick of that admittedly luscious hair.

"I don't spy anymore I'm just trying to be a better detective than I was a spy."

"I heard you held your own. Didn't the CIA want you at one time?"

"Only when they weren't convinced they could catch my mother."

"Did you really hand over your own mother?"

"That's just a nasty rumour. Do you dance?" Max had already got her on to the dance floor. She moved with his body with ease and pleasure. He would enjoy the next thirty-minutes or so with her and then return to his room without her. He hadn't always been this much in control. But now he wasn't needy. Despite the booze he was clear headed though he had to admit to himself she felt good.

He collapsed on the large double bed which was just what he needed, lots of space to stretch out, cool silky sheets, music softer now, less frenetic, people slowly going home to their loved ones, light coming through the blinds from a full moon and a cool breeze coming through the window he had opened as soon as he arrived. It felt like home more so than their tiny flat in London ever could. He still felt so alone at times. A sudden smile emerged on his face. He was drunk that's all.

***

Sean McBride had visited his sick mother and left Maddie tied up. He assured her as he left her that he would only be twenty-four hours at the most and he had to tie her up not because he thought she would escape but to convince his associates that she was indeed a hostage rather than his lover. He had reassured her that the photograph was necessary to further convince them he had taken the precautions necessary for a hostage. She had pleaded with him but was finally convinced as he took her beautiful face in his hands and wiped her tears away saying, "They will take you away from me if I don't prove to them you are my prisoner." Maddie paused a little too long for his liking but agreed to it, and her only concern was that she would wet herself before he returned.

"That doesn't matter Maddie it's only an old barn just straw and that will dry out quickly enough." And then he left. Left her in the dark. He had provided her with food and water and found a bucket before he left. As he posted the photo to her father he couldn't believe how she had believed him so totally. He loved her adoration. It made him feel good. He got back in his truck and drove back across the border undetected back home to the farm, the farm where he grew up. She had heard the bolt and the key locking it with the heavy chain and she had no fear. She decided to sleep as long as she could in the hope that he would be there when she woke up.

As he crossed the large open field of his family's farm he smirked to himself at the sheer naivety of this girl who was easy to deceive and a willing participant in just about anything he wanted her to do. Her falling in love with him was helpful and irritating at the same time. For such an expensively educated girl she could be very stupid. He had worried that she might realise why he pursued her, first of all at the local library in Hampstead near her school South Hampstead High; then the fancy tea and cake shop on the high street; then bumping into her on the Heath; then taking her for an illegal drink in the Gate House. He was her first sexual encounter of any kind. That part of their relationship was perfect. She seemed to love sex in a way the catholic girls would not allow themselves too. Even in the States he had to work too hard to get full intercourse but Maddie was different. It was a breeze.

"Is that you Sean?" His mother was sitting in her rocking chair by the open fire.

"You should stay in bed, Ma, that's what the doctor said." He rubbed her hands feeling how icy cold they were. Despite the warm spring, the house was still freezing and his mother was deteriorating at the relatively young age of seventy. He put two more logs on the fire and another blanket on her knees. He noticed her wispy grey hair needed washing and she smelled like she needed a bath but that kind of exposure might worsen her condition. The doctor put it down to grief.

"Your father is still warm in his grave." Sean had been furious at that remark. How long do these people train for and that's the only thing the family doctor could come up with?

"Why are you here, Sean?" his mother asked him with concern in her voice.

"To see you and make sure you'll be OK."

"Who is she, in the barn?" His mother sounded scared. "Why don't you bring her into the house so I could take a look at her, she might catch her death out there."

"Who told you about her, Ma?"

"That doesn't matter, bring her in. I want to meet her."

"That might not be a good idea."

"Why, 'cause she's one of them?"

Sean couldn't think of anything to say. He never lied to his mother. He was only short on the truth.

"She'll be no good to anyone, ill or worse." His mother chuckled but the seriousness of her words struck him. How the fuck did she know what he'd been up to. He hadn't even told her he'd been across the water.

"I'll make you some tea and give it some thought." Sean was unsure what to do next.

Could he risk bringing her in? The attic might do. She would still be hidden that might keep everyone happy. He would have to get permission. He would phone from the pub later. Still puzzling over how his ma knew every move he made, the kettle spilled over and he burnt his palm as he lifted it off the stove.

Max had sweaty palms and a stomach-ache. Katya was unimpressed. "Don't be such a wimp, it's just a hangover and besides you might be more convincing this way."

"In what way does a sick son become more convincing to his mother?"

"She'll feel that she has a role to play even for a short while."

"Do you know anything about my mother?" Max's tone made it clear he knew the answer.

"I read her file. She's had an interesting life. It's not very exotic anymore. I mean is it true about her and Che?"

"Probably, I wouldn't put anything past my mother!"

"Do you want to practice what you're going to say?"

"Nope, can you just drive and I'll try to get some sleep."

"Good idea, it's a long way."

"How long?"

"Two hours by road and then a little boat trip."

***

The barn door opened and as he stood there with the light behind him, his long curly hair looked almost blonde not the light brown the way she remembered it. She loved it when he tied it back and he would let her loosen it from the rubber band and pull it around into different shapes.

"Did you wet yourself?" he asked jokingly.

"You weren't away long enough." He untied her.

"I'm going to blindfold you and take you somewhere warm and more comfortable where you can wash and sleep in a bed."

She knew from this he must care a great deal for her.

***

"The infrastructure hasn't improved much under Castro." Max couldn't sleep; the roads were full of potholes and animals.

"No, the place is full of highly educated farmers who never get ill and if they do they have top class treatment in pristine hospitals whereas your average American could die on the street before receiving any treatment."

This was a dull discussion and one that held no interest for Max. His priority was to find a convincing way of lying to his mother not something that came easily to him.

They stopped overnight at a shabby but clean hotel run by a family whose hospitality was beyond the call of duty. He wondered if they were supported by CIA funds in return for services rendered. The two rooms had interlocking doors but when Katya came in uninvited she was fully dressed and to his relief made no obvious play for which he was grateful. He now always refused offers of the sexual kind but he found it difficult on occasions.

"Were you a good spy Max?" He wasn't expecting that.

"Not particularly. I only did it to spite my mother." He found it easy to talk to her.

"And Pablo?"

"Yes, him too. Though I eventually got over the sexual thing with my mother. In fact, that wasn't what bothered me, it was about how it changed our relationship. He was my adopted brother and that role satisfied me. He taught me many things about myself."

"Maybe it was just sex; why should that have upset you so much?" Katya was digging too deep.

"Fancy a Mojito before we head to our final destination?" He grabbed her hand and moved her into the Salsa pose.

"Oh, why not?" she giggled. She liked this man.

***

"Eeee, you poor wee girl stuck out in the barn. I bet you'd like a hot bath."

Maddie looked at Sean. "OK, Ma, if you want to fuss over the girl you can."

"Well if she's to be my daughter-in-law I want to see what she looks like when she's clean and ready to be seen. Now take her upstairs and show her where everything is."

"What's your mother on about?" Maddie felt an inner excitement and hoped he wouldn't avoid giving her an answer.

He looked her straight in the eyes. "My mother is ill and says the first thing that comes into her head. Now take your clothes off."

The attic was gloomy but clean and was a welcome improvement on the barn where she had spent at least ten days maybe more she couldn't recall. She had been used to a quiet residential part of North London. She had been used to regular meals, regular baths, regular reading and so on. This new life was feeding a craving in her life. She was wanted and loved and now she was ensconced in a more comfortable spacious place where her lover could spoil her. She missed her father but only now and again. She wanted this life or rather this man and everything it might offer with all the insecurity it might bring.

***

The boat trip was long despite the short distance between Cuba and Florida about ninety miles, he wasn't sure. Katya was talkative for a CIA agent telling him all about her husband and children. It all came as a surprise to him but he liked her more as she opened up. She admitted to missing them and always volunteered for the work not too far from home. She had been to the Middle East as they all had. It was a test of their nerve. She'd even fallen in love with a Mossad agent, the best sex she'd ever had.

They arrived somewhere in Florida. He was put in a car and blindfolded. This particular routine bored and irritated him.

She was facing the window with her back to him. The window was too high for her to see anything. He remembered her as tall but this woman must have shrunk over the years. How long had it been? Twenty-something years, yes, he was twenty-one and she was? Funnily enough he never knew her actual age. When she finally turned around he would never have recognised her. White hair cut short, stooped shoulders, very thin, too thin and lines drawn all over her face. She didn't smile. The room was tiny just enough room for a bed, a bucket and a small table with one chair.

"You can sit down if you like."

"Don't they give you anything to read?"

"Yes, I get a book a month."

"Don't they feed you, you're so thin?" She laughed and moved closer to him.

"You must remember Cuban cuisine?"

154

"We're not in Cuba."

"Well it was better than prison cuisine." This made him smile.

She smiled at him and said, "Why are you here, Max? A last mission from Soames?"

"I don't work for him anymore."

"Yes, you do. You've come to convince me you're still with your family so I'll give him the name he wants."

He knew she'd see through it.

"Did you see those ludicrous photos I was sent? Even I didn't manage those sex positions. Mind you, I wouldn't put it past you."

"So, my mission has failed then."

"Do you really think I care about who you are with? I'm never going to see my grandchildren or meet your ex-wife or your current wife. I wanted to see you."

***

"So, my handsome son, what are we to do with her?"

"I don't know yet. I haven't received orders but it's going too slowly if you ask me." Sean continued to fry the bacon.

"Does she like it crisp and burnt?"

"Yes, Ma."

"You're not getting fond of the girl, are you? You'll have to send her back one day and maybe even in a box!"

"Maybe, maybe not, that depends."

"On what?" His mother was clearly shocked at this.

"She says she believes in the cause."

"Don't be daft, Son, you're the only thing she wants for the moment and she'll see beyond that one day. Now don't be smoking us out or making me choke. You could never cook, not even a piece of toast."

Sean took up the bacon sandwich and enjoyed watching the fat drip down her chin.

She smiled up at him and he felt good just sitting there on the edge of the bed.

***

Max bribed the guard to let them out into the prison yard. This was the way in all prisons. She had shrunk so much she didn't reach his shoulder and she could barely walk but in the afternoon sunshine she began to come to life a little. It was pleasant and there was no hint of the humidity to come as early summer progressed into late summer when the mosquitos were so large they could almost knock you out as they hastened to find their next victim. But today the air was sweet. The surroundings needed some improvements. The small yard had a high white wall and on top was the electric fence. Max had almost forgotten the purpose of his visit.

"What's she like? Your Natalie?"

"She's complicated but I know I couldn't live without her. She took a long time to recover from Berlin."

"Will you ever be able to have children?"

"No, they had to remove the reproductive organs, they had been damaged and infected but they found that out too late."

"What had happened to Pablo to turn him into such a monster?"

"The Stasi."

"You know it may have begun long before they got him. When his sister, oh yes, he had an older sister who brought him to the house she intimated he'd been abused, rather brutally, I think. That's why I adopted him."

Max found himself startled by this information not wanting to hear anymore and he admitted to himself she could be lying as she had so often done in the past.

"I have enough children and I couldn't afford anymore. We live quite frugally, you know, a small flat in not a very desirable area of London but I'm hoping to earn enough from this case to move."

"I have money, Max, and I intend you should have it when I die."

Max was embarrassed by her openness.

"I know you think you don't want it but do you really want it to go to a dog's home? When the time comes, Soames will make the arrangements. He's a good man, always was, wanted to marry me once."

"You were lovers?" Somehow Max knew the answer to the question.

"Yes, he was my first handler."

"But not your first lover!"

"I know you always found that part of me hard to accept but your father was homosexual. Max, don't look so shocked, you must have known, deep down. Mind you I suppose I was rather promiscuous."

Max really couldn't think of anything to say. It all fell into place and he felt a strange warmth towards her in this moment, in this terrible place.

"Do you know the name I need for Soames and if so will you tell me."

"I will, but not today."

"What do you want from me?"

"I want to meet the woman who has made you so happy. I will tell her."

Max might have known she would continue to manipulate even at her age with nothing to live for. He took her back to her cell in silence.

"Goodbye, Mother."

"Goodbye, Max and tell Soames the window is too high for me to see the sea."

Max chuckled to himself.

Later that evening sitting at the bar Katya who had obviously taken some time on her appearance joined him. Her long hair was expertly now in a French plait, a style that had little appeal for him. He smiled to himself thinking back to the times when Natalie would experiment with wigs, sometimes at his request sometimes her own idea.

"So, she wouldn't squeak huh?"

"Nope."

"Did she want something else?"

"Nope."

"Do you want something else?"

He knew what she meant.

"Just to go home and as quickly as possible."

"OK, suit yourself. By the way that was a neat trick to get her outside so we couldn't hear anything."

"There was nothing to hear."

"If you say so." And Katya left knowing she would get nowhere with this man.

Max did go back early the next morning calling for a cab from the hotel lounge. Using his Spanish, he arranged to be picked up down the road half a mile from the hotel. Katya wasn't awake that early and her accomplice was actually asleep by the exit with a newspaper over his head. Again, it was bribery that got him in. She was still asleep, her cell was dark but the sun would break through, he reckoned in about five minutes. He watched her and wondered how much time she had left and how he hadn't hated her as he thought he would.

"Is that you?" she whispered.

"Yes. I came to say goodbye again."

The female guard looked through the grill and saw what she believed might have been some kind of reconciliation. They clasped hands briefly, then he got up and the guard opened the cell. She didn't look up as the guard locked her cell door, which slammed with a sound that seemed to shake the prison building. She led him through the first gate along the corridor. The next guard took over and again he was searched and again as he left. Before he left he gave the final guard an envelope for the governor of the prison. In the envelope there was a letter requesting a sea view and $500. He had already swallowed the piece of paper with the name on it. Her last words were "Judge for yourself when and to whom you should reveal this to."

He guessed he would never see her again.

***

"That was cheeky, Max." Katya smiled.

"What do you want to know?' Why are the CIA even interested in my visit to my dying mother?"

"Who told you she was dying?"

Katya didn't answer; she looked him straight in the eye and said, "You have to give me something for my report."

"Tell them, she had nothing to tell, you'll think of something. I've ordered a cab to the airport."

"It'll cost you a fortune, come with me I'll drive you."

"OK, just so long as we don't talk about our work."

"Just books then?"

"I don't read."

"Music?"

158

"As long as it's not opera."

**

"You've got a visitor, Sean." His mother still had a voice loud enough to make him jump.

"I'll be back but don't come downstairs Maddie." Sean kissed her tenderly. Something was changing and he felt some kind of panic in his throat.

"I'll be making you boys some tea, shall I?"

"No, Ma, we're down the pub for some discussions with the boys."

"Now, Sean, come here, let me tell you what to bring back for me."

He leaned over and the tall visitor decided to wait outside.

"Don't show your hand yet with the girl. They mustn't know anything. Tell them, she's still locked up in the barn if they ask. Bring me back a bottle, I don't have anything to keep me warm or help me sleep."

"Come on Sean, we can't keep him waiting any longer."

Sean was a good liar when necessary and had every confidence he could persuade them she would do anything for him. She had proved herself often enough. Crossing the border brought him out in a sweat but she played her part beautifully. She convinced the British Army she was on her honeymoon.

"Isn't he a bit old for you, love?" the soldier had said.

"I like mature men they know what to do in bed."

"You a virgin then?"

"Not anymore," she said.

Discoveries

"Did you get it?" Soames and Natalie asked in unison.

"Can I get in the car first, I'm freezing." Max had returned looking brown and relaxed but now he was freezing in the typical English summer.

"Which car?" Soames chuckled and Natalie simply raised her eyebrows.

"If you don't mind, Soames, I think I would prefer to go with my wife as you can imagine I've missed her greatly and she does have a way with me in cars." Natalie giggled.

"I'll give you two hours then come to the office." Soames was no longer seeing the funny side of the situation.

"I don't work for you anymore, Soames, so I'll come when I'm ready which may not be until tomorrow." He picked up his small black leather suitcase case in one hand and took Natalie's hand with the other. He gently squeezed it.

"Have you got jet lag, darling?"

"I have, so I may be up all night." They smiled at each other.

"How was your mother?" She got into the driver's seat while Max opened the boot and put his case in.

"She was ill, very thin, shrunken and rather sad."

"Well that's not at all surprising. How long has she been in prison?" Natalie was having trouble reversing out of the car park with two large black vehicles either side of the car.

"Do you want me to drive?"

"Would you, I seem to have messed up our exit." They changed places. They both noticed there were two men in one of the vehicles.

"Now who might this be? MI6? CIA?" Max looked straight at them.

"IRA?" Natalie joked.

"Well whoever they will be following us. Inevitable, they know where I've been."

"But do they know why you went?"

"Not unless there's a leak but I'm sure only us three know."

They drove quickly from Heathrow to home anxious to be together, alone but the car had followed them and parked itself across the street.

"Max maybe you should go and see Soames now he may be the one following us." She looked at the car but the men were not very visible from the flat.

"You need to tell him the name then it's his problem."

"I'm not going anywhere and I'm not telling him the name, now let's go to bed."

Afterwards Natalie's first words were "Well what's his name?"

"I'm not telling you the name. This is my mother's secret, and now it's mine."

Natalie understood the game. Soames would lose interest in the Belfast venture if he had the name and they would lose the support they needed.

"But how will you stall, you know he won't give up."

"I've got a little plan in my head. I will need you to adopt one of your disguises. But can we talk about this later as you have made me sleepy. I think we will eat out tonight. The food is dreadful in Cuba." He turned over and appeared to fall asleep immediately.

It was when she briefly hugged him in the warmth of the sun that she had whispered that Soames will have the information in his safe and knowing him the access code will be the same. The proof will be there and then the game is over.

"Don't worry, Soames will be absolutely fine, he has covered his tracks well, there won't be any evidence to convict him, only the Russian. He needs someone else to tell MI5 but he will take the credit. You must not do this yourself. Find someone you trust."

"Yes, I heard Hans had died. Soames told me – you mustn't come again and yes, I do love you and when she became distressed he felt the tears well up but her face changed. Go home and love and be loved, properly no lies, we lie too much in this business and it probably counts for very little in the end."

***

"Natalie, do you still have your cleaner's disguise, wig and all?"

"Yes but it's in storage."

"Well get it out and practice your working-class accent."

"Excuse me, Max, I am working class through and through, grammar school girl but true to my roots will never vote Tory. If I had my way I would happily assassinate Margaret myself."

"Leave that to the IRA." Max got out of bed and had a quick shower. He put on the cologne Natalie had bought for him, looked at himself in the mirror and noticed his dark hair exhibiting grey. He looked tanned but lined. He felt old.

"You smell nice." Natalie kissed his shoulders and played with his hair.

"I'm starving and need a substantial meal. Where do you fancy my darling?" Max carried on drying his hair.

"Let's go to China Town and get some sweet and sour king prawns. I'll call a cab."

They embraced. Natalie was glad to have him back. She had survived well on her own but now he was there she could relax and be herself. She had relied on her sleeping pills to get her to sleep otherwise every sound would have made her nervous. Max decided to drive and as expected they were followed.

"Let's hope they're hungry," Natalie remarked.

In China Town they walked hand in hand looking for a particular restaurant that Soames had recommended. He had phoned several times and when Max was ready to answer he teased Soames mercilessly.

"I need the name of the best Chinese restaurant in London," this was all Max would say. Soames reluctantly gave him the information. "I need to see you Max, tomorrow."

"Should I come with your fellows outside?" Max heard the pause, which told him they were nothing to do with the British Intelligence Services.

"I will pick you up myself, Max."

"Don't make it too early as I need to attend to my lady."

Natalie wasn't sure she liked this information sharing but couldn't help smiling.

"You know what they say about Chinese food."

162

"Yes Max, it fills you up briefly and then you're hungry again." Natalie was unbearably happy looking at this divinely handsome man. She felt like a child. Still only in her twenties she decided this was entirely acceptable.

"I hope they like Chinese food." Max stopped using chopsticks and asked the waiter for a fork.

"Well I'm guessing not if they're Russian," Natalie mused.

"I'm guessing yes if they're Americans." Max was a little more serious than he had intended to be.

Natalie took the opportunity to probe, "What's going on Max? I know you have the name and won't tell me for my own protection but why am I breaking into Soames' safe, and photographing a file called Oasis?"

"Because I'm instructing you to and as soon as I can tell you everything, I will."

He leant forward and looked in to the green eyes he so adored and said, "You must trust me on this, it's so potentially cataclysmic." The fork arrived and finally Max was able to eat and he was hungry.

Max drove home as Natalie had had too much to drink. She had become less afraid of driving but she still preferred Max to drive at night.

"When do I do this?"

"Tomorrow night, no point in prolonging the mission."

***

Sean McBride covered his nervousness well. A pint of Guinness helped him relax as he met the regional commander simply referred to as the general. He was a broad-shouldered man though not tall still imposing and capable of commanding the loyalty of some very violent men. His light-red hair was beginning to turn a powdery grey. Sean had learnt to be scared of him from a very early age and although he was a good friend of his father's, Sean couldn't forgive him for sending his father across the border with his weak heart.

"We're reactivating the campaign and I want you by my side young Sean. I want your promise that this girl will get her father over here soon, very soon, are yer understanding what I'm saying?"

"Yes, I have a plan."

"And what is it?"

"She's fallen in love with me."

The general laughed, as did the two men who were obviously his bodyguards.

"Well, you always were for the ladies I recall and yer surely the most good-looking man I know. Course she's fallen for you. I'd expect no less. But what's the plan?"

"I'll offer to marry her and draw her father over to stop the marriage."

There was a long pause. The general leant back against the back of the wooden chair. "Tommy, get another round, will yer take your time. Cillian go get some fresh air." When they had cleared the small room set away from the main pub, the commander leaned forward and said quietly, "Explain yourself."

Sean knew he had one chance to convince this man.

"You know, Sean, I was always a bit romantic myself but you know what you have to do and once it's over even if you win her to our cause."

"I know."

"And can you get the one we're really after to come with him?"

"Yes, that's going to be easy."

"Oh, really?"

"Now stay for another and relax a little like old times and tell me just how easy your plan is to make happen."

He wasn't followed from the pub. It was dark; many stars appeared in the clear sky. He wished he had gone back to New York after his father's funeral. He wished he had never met Maddie, he wished he had never agreed to the mission, he wished he could disappear. He heard her calling gently from the attic like some Juliet on a balcony. His mother was already asleep. He brought Maddie down the stairs and sat her on his lap in front of the dying fire.

"Will you marry me?"

She kissed him long and hard.

"You must let your father know and get him to bring along a friend. We don't want him to be sad at our wedding losing his darling girl now do we?"

"I look ridiculous, Max."

"That's the idea, totally unrecognisable but a plausible replacement for the current, very sick, cleaner. She's already told everyone she has a fever and her sister Sharon will do her shift."

"How did you persuade her to betray her country?"

Max started playing with the wig, pulling a few strands, "It's a bit curly isn't it? Don't forget, I used to work there and I'm very good with the working classes."

Natalie pretended this comment didn't bother her and simply said, "How much did it cost you?"

"It cost Matthew £100."

"Is that all?"

"No, you get £500 if you're successful and I get £1000 if all goes to plan." Max slapped her on the bottom. "Just getting you into role."

"Put that big fur coat on so no one sees what we are up to." As Natalie put on the coat that cost her £10 at Camden Market she felt a sudden panic but disguised her fear and said, "How are we going to shake off the lads?"

"Don't worry, I have a plan."

Natalie retorted, "Of course you do."

Matthew was in shock and called Max straightaway.

"She's going to marry him and they want me to go to the wedding."

"When? When is the wedding Matthew?"

"She didn't say. I thought she had been kidnapped for money now she is going to marry an IRA terrorist. How does that happen?"

Max sat down next to Natalie who was still combing her wig affectionately. The sofa was small and uncomfortable for two; he thought he couldn't wait to buy a bigger one.

"Matthew, it doesn't. I think it's a ruse to get you over there."

"But why would they want a retired industrialist?" Matthew sounded frantic.

Max was calm but stern in his reply, "Matthew, I have been waiting for you to offer some kind of explanation. Sit down, calm down and do some thinking instead of drinking. Natalie and I have some work to do connected to the case but I will phone you first thing and I hope you have some ideas by then. Goodnight."

"That's a little harsh." Natalie had the wig back on.

"I think he's been holding something back. This new development will shake him up a little."

There was a knock on the door and a man and a woman entered. Natalie didn't know either of them. Max gave them the car keys. "Now wait until we have gone then, arm in arm, kiss then get into our car and drive an hour at least before you stop then make love in the car then drive on for another hour. Then drive slowly back. That should give us enough time. Give me your keys."

Natalie followed Max down the stairs through the back way into the small garden. It was late enough to be dark she thought about nine. Summer was on its way, she could smell some jasmine. They went down the side lane and into a strange car. She took no interest in the makes of cars but she noticed how comfortable it was to sit in leather seats. There was a radio, which she hastily put on to calm her nerves. Donna Summer 'Hot Stuff', hardly calming music more disco but it would do.

"Who were they?"

"Mates of mine, from the old days."

"Will they really make love in our car?"

"Probably." Max put some black-rimmed glasses on which he now needed for driving at night. His hair was now so long it sat easily off his forehead and behind his ears.

"OK, Natalie, check the camera. Take a picture of me if you like."

"It's fine, it still works I took a picture of your friends."

They drove off to Soames' office.

***

Maddie and Sean were already in his bed. After checking on his mother gently snoring in her bed he returned to Maddie and got her to phone her father after which he wiped away her tears and took her back upstairs and held her till she fell asleep in his arms. He was content lying next to her stroking her long curly hair. In the morning Maddie cried as she said, "He won't come."

"He'll get use to the idea, Sean reassured her."

"But I don't think he'll come to the wedding."

"Well you must persuade him, tell him you're pregnant and he's going to be a grandfather, surely that'll make him happy."

"I can't lie to him."

"Yes, you can," Sean said firmly.

***

"The door's stuck. I can't even get in the bloody office."

"Go back to security and say it's the wrong key or something and try not to use the pager, it's too noisy." At that moment the key worked and Natalie was in. She had memorised the access code and the safe opened easily enough. The security guard came in at that very moment. "So, what's the matter with Shirl?" Natalie stood still in front of the safe frozen.

"Oh, I see," he continued, "your sister doesn't want anyone to know. That's OK, I won't tell anyone, her secret's safe with me."

"Good, good I know she'll appreciate that." They stood facing each other.

"Don't mind me asking, but is that a wig you have on?"

"Yes, yes, it is, thank you but I need to get on I've all this floor to finish."

"All right love but don't forget to say goodnight and give my love to Shirl."

She had no trouble opening the safe, Rebecca had been right, Soames hadn't changed the code. Natalie had wondered how Max's mother had known it in the first place. She would ask Max on the way home.

The file Oasis was underneath all the other paperwork. She daren't get it out but photographed it page by page while it was still in the safe. With a small torch in her mouth there was enough light. There were fifteen pages double sided in illegible handwriting. On leaving Soames' office she managed to avoid the security guard and Max was close to the exit of the building just where he said he would be.

Back in the car the sweat poured off Natalie. He drove quickly away as Natalie ripped the fur coat off and swore she would never wear it again. She opened the window and threw it out the car. Max was never surprised by anything she did.

"Well done," Max said, "Are you OK?"

"Yes, it was surprisingly easy."

"Will he suspect?"

"I hope so, that's our bargaining chip."

"Fancy a drink? You can keep the wig on."

She tugged at it for several minutes; the grips had dug into her head but finally with a joyful yelp that too got flung out of the window.

"Looking like this? No thank you. Let's go home." They were back before all the strangers. Natalie went for a bath and Max tried to work out the next move.

There was really only one option, to go to Belfast with Matthew for the wedding. The file Oasis would keep Soames on their side and secure his cooperation. His only worry was if his mother was telling the truth. It was a serious accusation. With that anxiety he had a restless night and was happy to see the light coming through their bedroom window. First Matthew, then Soames.

"There's something you're not telling me, Matthew, and I can't promise a successful outcome unless you tell me. You know why they took your daughter and why."

Matthew was now walking slowly over to the mantelpiece where there was a photo of his wife who had passed away for a number of years.

"She was Irish you know, my wife. I met her there when I opened the factory and we had a residence there."

"Go on, Matthew, the whole story please." Max felt this was the opportunity and he had to press hard.

"I was very much in love with her, Max. But I'm not that interested in politics. I was good at making money. I never doubted her love and allowed her access to anything she asked for. At first it was only to come in and help in the factory, be a kind of secretary. I had no idea why she wanted to work. She made me laugh, she said she wanted to keep an eye on me, she didn't want me to have a secretary in case we had an affair."

He was shaking.

"She fooled me for a long time. She pretended, you know in bed and all that sort of thing and all the time she was IRA." He spat the words out. "But then when she got pregnant she was sick, very sick all she could do was stay at home and rest, she didn't

168

want to. I still wasn't suspicious and then I got in someone without telling her to look at the books and you can guess the rest. Money was being diverted into an account, a false account. I still didn't put two and two together and when Maddie was born I was distracted. I wouldn't believe she could do wrong especially now she was a mother."

"And do you know how I found out? I followed her one day, right into the fucking Falls Road. She left the baby with the nanny and sneaked out. She didn't know I was in, she thought I had already left for the factory. I must have looked out of place with everyone staring at me. I felt their suspicion. I watched her go into a house, one of those disgusting little houses at the back of which there would be alleyways and washing hung out. There alongside the outside toilets little, dirty children would play football. I waited for an hour in the pouring rain and when she emerged she was flushed and happy with her hair down round her shoulders. The man was drawing her back in with his arms, kissing her neck and then her lips. I had never seen passion like that. I envied it, I loathed it, I wanted it, from her. In that moment my stupidity hit me in the face. I was twenty years older than her. I wasn't even handsome."

Max felt sorry for him but still knew there was more. Matthew continued, "I went to see Soames and told him what I had discovered. He was sympathetic but excited. He devised a plan. I was to allow her back to work for me, he would have her followed and all I had to do was act as if nothing had happened. I never tried to make love to her again although Soames encouraged me to try in case she got suspicious. The operation was known as Sunflower; God knows where they get their names."

He sat down but then got straight up again.

"They followed her to the bank where the account was held, the bank manager had tipped them off. The bank manager was instructed to ask her to return in the afternoon while they counted the money. She went to her lover and returned at the appointed time to the bank." He paused. Max saw the pain in his face.

"They watched her take the money, place it in a shopping bag and leave. A woman with a pram with no baby placed the shopping bag in the pram and walked back to her house and my wife returned to her lover."

Max was losing patience with the man and the story, Matthew must have sensed this. He looked Max and continued.

"It ended badly, the woman pushing the pram tried to run they shot her. They raided the house where my wife was making love. They shot them both while they were in bed. That's when I left Belfast with my daughter, the very next day in fact."

Matthew started crying. There was silence for a while.

"Look, Matthew, I'm going to see Soames. I have some questions for him. I'll get back to you later. Tell your daughter you will be at her wedding."

Soames wore a grim expression on his round face. He put his glasses on and stared at Max as if he could kill him.

"So, your mother tells you I'm a traitor and you believe it."

"Not necessarily but I have a copy of the file safely hidden to ensure your support in getting Maddie back."

"Christ! Max, I could have you incarcerated for this."

Soames broke the silence, "How's Natalie?"

"She's fine, she photocopied the file, very slick job and she's coming with me to Belfast."

"To the wedding?" Soames got up and walked to the window "And what's the plan? To kidnap her back?"

"Well Natalie will play a large part in disillusioning the girl about her IRA boyfriend and if that isn't enough, yes is the answer to your question. That's all Matthew wants. But on the way we will try to find out what Sean McBride is planning and pass everything on to you."

"The Natalie thing with Craig and the photos I'm rather sorry about that." Soames looked genuinely sorry.

"Well Natalie will be using it in reverse with Sean, she looks upon it as therapy." Max smiled. But, of course, he had already articulated it to Natalie some time ago. He was interested if Soames felt the same.

"And the other thing?" Soames had desperation in his voice.

Max smiled. "Oh don't worry you'll go out with a bang."

"OK Max, you hold all the cards. I guess I'll have to trust you. Try not to get discovered, it won't be nice if you do."

"Tell me a little more about Matthew's wife."

"It was a fucking mess." Soames went to his drawer where he kept the whisky.

"Everyone got bloody shot." Soames poured two glasses and sat down.

"Why was that?" Max took a sip – he couldn't resist the quality of Soames' whisky.

"Well the woman with the pram just ran and the wife's lover pulled a gun – had it under the pillow. The soldiers were young, inexperienced – they were meant to go in and arrest them but they panicked, training wasn't good in those early days much better now." Soames was already on his second glass.

"The marriage was a trap. She was IRA from the start, born and bred. Matthew was so besotted; he married her within a fortnight. I'd lost contact with him for a while otherwise I would have spotted the signs. Actually, it could have been very useful to us I would have found a few more of the bastards before they could do any real damage."

"What are they after now do you suppose? The factory's gone, they haven't asked for money – he's going to marry her?"

"Well if it's not money it'll be information or a trap or both?" Soames leaned forward.

"He knows some minor Royalty. They may be interested in that angle." Soames sat back in his comfortable leather chair that had been the envy of the office.

"You're not suggesting—" Soames interrupted him before he could articulate his thought.

"It's gone quiet, they want to rejuvenate the war and if they get a royal even a minor one," Soames sighed

"At the wedding?" Max hoped he was wrong.

"That's where I'd do it if I wanted to start a war with the British," Soames said in his matter of fact way.

"Jesus Christ! I don't think Matthew will be inviting anyone." Max was trying to reassure himself.

Soames laughed out loud. "Matthew isn't very bright you know, Max. I saw him last night at the club and he is ensuring that his beloved daughter has the best possible wedding. He's providing a large sum of money for her to splash out on caterers and so on." Soames poured Max another drink.

"What's your cover story? Another honeymoon?"

"No, I'm an investor, she will be my PA and so on. Will the same team be with us over there?"

"The ones outside your flat? No, they're too inexperienced. Don't worry I'll keep you safe – I still need that name. I don't suppose?" Soames didn't finish the question.

They both raised their glasses and smiled. There had been a kind of reconciliation.

They understood the world they had been part of and both wanted out of and this was the way. Soames retires and with that Max loses his contact with the service. They make enough money to survive on their own terms.

As Max drove home he had a devastating thought – supposing Matthew didn't have the money he promised. I must check this before I even get the plane tickets.

Natalie had already packed her case as Max discovered when he tripped over it in their tiny hallway.

"Christ, we need to move," he said out loud but the flat was empty. He was thankful that this no longer made him anxious. She really had turned the corner. How odd that was, as Hans hadn't been gone that long. Maybe that was it. While he was alive how could she heal? He flopped on their bed and dozed. Too much whisky too early in the day.

Soames had always thought he should take better care of that file. He should have burned it. He was once her handler and her lover; Rebecca was now an agent for the Russians. He remembered sleeping with her once, only once in her Cuban home. Her son Max was downstairs with his adopted brother, the arrogant Pablo who took his place as her lover. Oasis was an operation that went so badly wrong even more wrong than Berlin. Somewhere in that file was the name of the double agent. He would study it when he was sober. There was a whole network of agents, it was a huge operation but he was drunk and tired, tired of it all, too tired to care enough to find the name. Let Max find it for him. He called a cab and left the office to go home to beloved Yolanda. But he went to the bathroom and cleaned his teeth. He wondered if she was fooled or just decided to let it go. Whisky had been his love for many years before her and he couldn't give it up.

Celebrations

"Do you have to pack so much?" Max asked Natalie.

"What do you mean? We don't know how long we're going to be there, do we?"

He didn't answer which led her to believe he did but wasn't saying.

After a moment he said, "Why don't you buy over there?"

"Because the shops are hardly ever open and when they are they're being blown up."

He didn't answer.

"Do we have to come back to this place, Max?"

He didn't answer. He wasn't going to spoil the surprise.

He had the cover story worked out in sufficient detail but as a rule or rather it was tradition, in his mind anyway to use plane time to absorb the cover. But the flight was short so he gave her the folder the previous evening. She liked it apart from the married part. She wanted to be his mistress not his wife; his P/A not his companion; American and blonde not an English Rose; flirtatious not shy; a vegetarian Jew not an atheist meat-eater. Max went along with her changes and felt a pleasure in her confidence that she would make it work. Max had procured a substantial deposit for the job and he had already put it towards that house in Hampstead but Matthew had gone further than that. He had promised his own house if he himself did not return on the condition they adopted his daughter and ensured she had a safe future. Max was reluctant to agree to these terms and hoped none of this would be necessary. He rather liked the house but he already had his own problem daughter without adopting another but he signed the contract anyway and as the cab arrived his last wish was that they all came back safely.

***

Sean told his mother the marriage could be easily annulled but it was necessary to hire the church and have a genuine Catholic wedding.

"I can't go along with this," his mother was adamant. Thankfully, he thought Maddie was still fast asleep and wouldn't overhear.

"I'll have her shot before I let you annul the marriage," she screeched at him.

"Well that solves the problem then."

"Where are you going now, Sean?"

"I have things to do and when Maddie wakes up be nice." He slammed the kitchen door behind him. A car was waiting for him. The meeting was set up and the plan was going ahead. When Sean arrived at the small pub he headed for the back room but it was empty. The young lad serving behind the bar in the public area didn't give anything away and Sean ordered a Guinness. He didn't have to wait long for the General and his bodyguards and he followed them into the back room waiting to be told to sit down. What he heard in that room shook him. The changed plan wasn't to his liking but it was war and he raised no objection at the time and as the time of the plan's execution grew closer he had come to terms with it.

He returned home and saw Maddie had eaten and probably gone for a walk, as it was the beginning of what was to be an unusually warm summer. He looked across the field and wished he had never returned from America. It was a mess, the sort of mess Israel and Palestine were in, maybe not as unresolvable but it seemed that way, unresolvable while men like the General were in charge. There were men who could see no way out other than violence, they wanted it that way and he Sean hadn't the energy or strength of character to change things. He looked now to the future, they promised him he could return to the States as soon as it was over. He would have to, as he would be a fugitive. He smiled just at the moment Maddie came into view and she thought, he really does love me.

***

"It's only a short flight so maybe alcohol on an empty stomach isn't such a good idea?"

"Darling, that's when it is a good idea. It goes straight to the head." Natalie smiled as she ordered a large gin and tonic.

"You must stop worrying, I've got it under control but flying makes me nervous so cut me a bit of slack will you, Max?"

"You want to be more nervous about our hotel," Max looked down at Heathrow Airport.

"The Europa? It looks very nice." Natalie leant across him but decided to retreat quickly from looking out the window as they were still climbing and it made her anxious.

"You haven't done your research then?" Max was still looking out of the window.

"Yes, I have but I figured that if the wedding reception is there the IRA wouldn't bomb it that particular day at least. Where's that gin?"

"They have to wait until it's safe for them to get out of their seats." He grabbed her hand, she was shaking. She leant back and closed her eyes marvelling at the fact he always got it right. Not too much fuss, no hint of impatience. If he ever left her she would kill him or herself or both of them somehow, stupid thoughts, a crazy moment. She had brought Han's journal with her but it gripped her less and less.

Matthew was on the other side of her. He hadn't said a word for some time. Her heart went out to this man who had lost his wife whom he loved and now his daughter who of all things was marrying an IRA gunman old enough to be her father, well almost.

There had been no demands made for money, which was odd, just an invitation to his daughter's wedding. The gin and tonic arrived and Matthew ordered whisky but Max had nothing. He was looking again at the file on Sean McBride. It was all there, the facts but nothing about the man himself. He had returned from the States for his father's funeral but he had previously been on the periphery never a man to be on the frontline, never military. Max wondered why he didn't simply return to the States and carry on raising money for the Cause. Why get so involved?

Natalie stroked his thigh; she always became amorous at inappropriate moments. He took her hand away and kissed her fingertips one by one. The first night in the hotel would be theirs. The landing was good, the car was waiting for them and they went straight to the hotel and all three went straight to their rooms. When Max and Natalie went downstairs to dinner they saw Matthew was already seated at the table with his daughter and Sean. Natalie noted how good-looking Sean was, in the same way as Max, dark wavy hair, deep brown eyes, a perfect profile, a strong nose, lips not too thick, not too thin.

"I'd like you to meet my business associate and his Personal Assistant who are with me first as guests but are looking into an investment I'm interested in making." Matthew was totally convincing.

"I'm delighted to meet you both." Natalie noticed how he looked at her. His voice was soft, his accent not as strong as expected but then he had lived a long time in America. Maddie's insecurity caused her to grab Sean's hand. She looked vulnerable and her eyes darted from Sean to Matthew but she managed to speak.

"Are you coming to the wedding?" She looked at Natalie.

"Well we hadn't planned to," Natalie spoke quickly.

"Oh, you must." Sean smiled. "Why don't you join us here? You must be hungry."

"I'm afraid my PA and I have much to talk over before our meeting tomorrow so we will be eating on our own, but thanks." Max moved away but Sean gently grabbed his arm. "You didn't say about the wedding, whether you're coming or not."

"I honestly don't think we can spare the time," Max said cheerfully.

"Well the reception then, after all you're staying here so you can just pop down from your room, rooms rather," Sean corrected himself with an ironic smile.

Natalie responded this time, "It'll be a pleasure."

As they sat at a table, Max said sourly, "I expect the food's terrible."

"Max, you haven't even looked at the menu. What's the matter?"

"You're attracted to him, aren't you?"

"Only because he looks like you…" Having seen Max's expression, she quickly qualified it her remark, "you know, dark-brown eyes, good mouth. Perhaps we should cancel the plan?"

"Certainly not, the room's being set up at this very moment, we only have tonight and tomorrow so with my permission you can start the routine right now."

"We'll have to swap places then because I'm in Maddie's sight."

They moved places and as they did so they kissed. Sean had noticed.

After a weak gin and tonic, Max looked at the menu and Natalie looked around the dining room. She had noticed the evidence of bomb blasts at the front and back of the hotel but now noticed a hole behind a rather beautiful screen, the kind she had always loved. Probably a total fake but the screen looked silk with delicately painted birds, light brushstrokes and milky colours.

"I think we should move tonight while the iron's hot, so to speak."

"Well that would cut the cost for Soames."

"You need to get Maddie and Matthew away as soon as they finish eating and then I'll make my move."

"Be careful, darling. He's no fool." Max kissed her hand.

"Max, I was thinking. Why would Sean organise his wedding reception in the most bombed hotel in Europe?"

"By the IRA, Natalie, so it's a reasonable assumption they won't be blowing up one of their most useful soldiers."

"Unless he doesn't plan to be here at his own wedding reception."

"Yes, you're brilliant that's the plan. It must be."

"Hang on, Max, it's just a theory."

The meal arrived but they had both lost their appetite. Max ordered more gin for Natalie and whisky for himself. They didn't want to be apart that night. They needed to talk and think and sleep.

"We wait until tomorrow night."

"I'll spend all day tomorrow grooming him. It can wait until tomorrow evening, better to wait. Take Matthew and Maddie away for the day and leave Sean to me."

"Do I need to worry?" Max suddenly looked and sounded vulnerable.

They rose from the table and as they passed by the table where Maddie, Matthew and Sean were sitting she took Max's hand and looked directly at Sean as she said, "We'll see you all tomorrow."

Sean twitched as he watched them resenting their intimacy. He was too used to being at the centre of any female's attention whether it be his mother or mistress. He thought she was very attractive but his thoughts were distracted as Maddie eased her hand into his.

Max and Natalie had booked separate rooms. They went to his. They had no intention of being filmed. They both knew Soames had watched all such recordings even with his new Italian wife he never delegated this part of the job.

The single room had a single bed, which was fun for making love but not for sleeping in. Natalie woke up and needed the toilet. En-suite bathrooms didn't seem to feature in Ireland and so she put on her black silk dressing gown, which Max had bought her from Harrods. It wasn't really warm enough for early summer in Ireland but she felt good in it. On returning from what seemed like a very long, cold corridor she was shivering.

"Come here and let me warm you." The voice that she knew so well seemed strange in the total silence and darkness.

"Why is this city so quiet?"

Max joked with her, "You mean when the bombs aren't going off." He rubbed her gently. "There's still a curfew, even though the bombing campaign has been suspended."

She got out of bed and sat at the desk. *Strange*, she thought *there's a desk and lamp but no toilet just a tiny sink useless to wash properly in.* She got Han's journal out of her suitcase. Max had already turned over and was probably on the edge of sleep.

She had already read it a couple of times but she would often dip into it. She knew the page she wanted to re-read. It felt like after this she might even leave it behind. But maybe one last read of this particular page.

I liked her straightaway. She looked and acted natural. I had never known anyone who looked so pleased to see me. Of course, it was more to do with the knowledge that she would soon be with Max again but somehow that didn't matter. She talked so openly about her feelings, her friends and anything else that came into her head. She was so positive about the future never gloomy wanting to have fun but in a responsible way.

I had kept away from women most of my life and as a fitness freak I didn't like anyone to drink or smoke especially women but with Natalie it felt acceptable even likeable.

She isn't beautiful in the true classic sense but she is beautifully attractive. She is stylish without having to spend too much money. She has an eye for what looks good on her. She would accuse me of being sexist if she could read this but then she never will. The first time I realised I was in love with her was that night that neither of us can speak about. I thought she might die. I hoped I would but I wanted her to live and love, Max of course. But will he stay with her; will he make sure she can be happy again?

I'm dead inside and out. When she comes to see me, I am ashamed and guilty. It was my fault. They keep telling me Pablo had become a monster and no one knew not even Max. He had disappeared, off the radar for months. We were to bring him in, to protect him. But someone must have known. I know someone must have known the state he was in...

Natalie thought to herself that he must have fallen asleep and yet the next entry was the next day.

My nurse has just left. She has washed me, a thorough wash today. She turned me over too quickly and hurt my legs even though the nerves are all dead I still feel pain.

She has emptied my bags and replaced them. She will return soon with my breakfast.

She will smile and bring in an orderly and between them they will put me in my wheelchair. When I have finished breakfast, they will take me in the lift out into the park and round the lake.

I hate that lake...

She wants me to live with them. I once would have liked that but not now, Now I want to die so very much but they won't let me but I have a plan and I know how to be patient. Day by day, slowly...

I have discovered I'm not patient now I have made the decision I must hurry. I have enough pills I have more than enough...

I will see her one more time when she is alone not with Max and I will tell her it's for the best, it's what I want.

"You must be getting cold, come back to bed."

"Yes, I will, I am shivering."

"Max, have you ever wondered why Hans wrote his journal in English not German?"

"So you could read it, and he also hated all things German, now get some sleep."

Morning arrived too quickly for both of them.

Natalie who hadn't slept at all spoke softly, "He's no fool, what if he doesn't go for it."

"We only have a couple of days before the wedding, we can find another way." Max didn't sound convincing.

"We could kidnap her back?" Natalie pulled a face and Max got out of bed grumpy with backache choosing to ignore her last suggestion.

"Have a shower and doll yourself up, today will be better."

***

Soames got out of bed leaving his wife Yolanda snoring. He would go into his office to keep an eye on operations. He sincerely hoped this was the end for him. He wanted this to be over. He wanted the name of the Russian agent, he wanted never to see Max again and he wanted to retire in Italy with his Italian wife basking in the glory of his revelation. He might even get an OBE for his services to the Intelligence Agency he had given his life to. He reminded himself of his failures with Max's mother Rebecca, with Max's mistress now wife Natalie and the Berlin debacle and one of his best agents Hans who acted without instruction that day. Now he and Max were once again entwined in a risky mission.

Alice, Max's ex-wife couldn't get hold of Max to tell him their eldest daughter Alex had run away again so she rang Soames who heard the phone ringing in his office. He unlocked the door hastily hoping to hear from Max but picked it up to hear Alice's distressed voice.

"Where is he?"

"Who is this?" Soames was stalling in order to get his story straight. He knew this voice having often made up lies about Max's whereabouts so often in the past.

"He's in the Lake District with Natalie, having a short break."

"Give me the telephone number of where they're staying. He needs to find Alex."

"What, again?"

"Christ! Soames, try to be a little more understanding." Alice did sound very upset.

"Alice, I will try and get in touch with him but why don't you let me help?"

"Because he's her father not you but you can pass on the message as I don't particularly want to speak to him." She put the phone down.

He wasn't going to contact Max, he was busy but Craig wasn't so he called him in.

"You found her before so find her again and take her home to her mother. And let me know as soon as it's done."

Craig didn't answer, he didn't have to, as he felt it was below his rank to go finding missing teenagers but he was good at finding people, it was a knack. He knew London like the back of his hand and he was sure he could find her again.

Natalie had showered in a freezing cold bathroom next to the toilet she had used in the middle of the night and had gone down to breakfast alone as planned. Matthew had already gone shopping with Maddie for her trousseau as planned and Max left the hotel as planned. Sean was already in the dining room reading a newspaper. He became aware of her as she sat down at a table by the window. Neither of them moved. She ordered coffee and toast. He waited and she waited. When she finished breakfast, she left the table walking past him and he looked up and said, "Good Morning. What are your plans today?"

"I don't have any."

"Where's your boss?"

"He doesn't need me today. Where's your fiancé?"

"She's gone shopping with her rich daddy."

He stood up as if to follow her.

"Would you like me to show you Belfast?"

"Okay, as we are both alone, how long will it take?"

"As long as you want, a couple of hours then back here for lunch."

"I didn't sleep well so I'll probably just want to go to bed after that." Natalie tried not to make this sound too flirtatious.

"I'll get my coat."

Sean smiled, he was handsome and he knew it.

He followed her up to her room and waited outside the door.

As they left the hotel Max decided to follow them.

"You're not going to try to convert me to the cause, are you?" Natalie wondered if this was the right approach with this man but as always trusted her instinct.

"Hell no, why the fuck should I do that?" Sean warmed his hands by blowing hard on them.

"Are you cold?"

"I have poor circulation and I prefer warmer climates."

"Ah yes you lived in New York for years, didn't you?"

"How come you know so much about me?"

"Max works for your future father-in-law."

"Oh yes, I almost forgot."

Natalie thought he was a poor liar.

"Let me take you to the heart of IRA territory."

"Will I be safe?" Natalie played the naive card.

"Of course, you're with me."

***

Craig was demented – he had worn himself out looking for the girl Alex and having looked in all the usual homeless areas he decided to go home without phoning Soames with whom he had become disenchanted. No promotion, no prospects, no recommendations and Soames gone by Christmas probably with an excellent pension. His resentment had festered and his exclusion from the current episode in Ireland had made him feel like going to Soames' superior and spilling the beans. Soames was using MI5 resources to get back a friend's kidnapped daughter. He had employed Max – an ex-agent to run the operation for financial rewards and in return Soames gets the name of a Russian agent working under deep cover in MI6 which an ex-double agent, now incarcerated in an American prison who happens to be the mother of Max gave to her son as a farewell present before she dies. You couldn't have made it up he thought as he walked home. He had also reliable information that the IRA was involved in some way but he needed to figure that out before going any further.

He would go in early and search through Soames' files providing he hadn't remembered to put them in the safe. He often forgot, he was definitely too old for the job now.

***

Belfast reminded Natalie of Berlin, dirty divided, graffiti everywhere, rubbish everywhere. The streets were quiet apart from the armoured vehicles, bullet proof, with small openings behind which British soldiers sat with their rifles waiting for moments of violence, ready to kill. This world was as strange to her as Berlin had been.

"Do you like my home?"

"Of course not, it reminds me of Berlin."

"And the British are to blame for that too."

"I suppose you have a point."

"You know I do."

"But apportioning blame may not help to find a solution."

"You're right there, Natalie, but it gets you through the day, it gives you focus and sometimes it even makes you feel good to punish."

"Do you know the history of this place, Natalie, and why we want it?"

"You want a united Ireland and that's impossible so you're bombing and killing and getting nowhere."

"Let me show the Catholic Falls road and the way they have to live, it's a ghetto." When they reached the Divas flats the hardship was obvious but Natalie felt detached because this was such an obvious tactic. It was the wall that made her shake and brought the bile up to her throat.

"Get me out of here, I'm not interested in your cause, I don't care Sean I really don't and do you know what else I'm not sure you do."

"Who the fuck are you?"

"I'm with Max on a business trip accompanying Matthew but you already know that."

"Why is he following us?"

"Look this is not turning out well so why don't we just return to the hotel. I am sensing you're agitated because I can't condone your tactics."

"But what about our intentions?"

"I don't have a view I really don't care. Like most English people as long as you don't harm us why should we?"

"That'll come you know, the bombs in London only next time there'll be no warnings."

"Can we go back to the hotel please?"

"You know that hotel is a target, our favourite target."

"Why are you having your reception there?"

"Because it's safe for me, and when the wedding's over I will return to New York a happy man."

"You don't love her, do you?"

"Actually, I'm very fond of her and I reckon we could be quite happy if we get the chance." They stopped at a mural, there were many on the walls of Belfast.

"Did they have these in Berlin?"

Natalie shuddered.

"What happened to you in Berlin?" She almost fainted and Sean had to hold on to her as he guided her to a small wooden bench.

"Your man is looking anxious so I'm going to cut the tour short and let him take over. Will I catch you later in the bar maybe?" And he was gone.

"Jesus, Max what's happening here?"

"Frankly Natalie this is beginning to feel like insanity."

"Yes, he's on to us and I get the impression he's not staying around for the wedding."

"So it's imperative you get more out of him."

"He wants to meet in the bar later and I think that's the time to put the plan into action."

"Maddie will be out of the way dining with Matthew and his royal friend."

It was like one of those moments in life rare as they are when everything seems to fall into place so obvious and yet still not quite believable.

"So how will they do it and where?" Natalie spoke the words.

"Not in the church but at the reception – a bomb inside or a car bomb outside? Do you think you can find out?"

"I can try."

They hugged each other in the Catholic ghetto surrounded by a wall separating the two sides. A place where a civil war was happening and so few people outside seemed to care.

Sean had hinted at the future though he didn't want to be part of it nevertheless was going to participate in some kind of atrocity. Natalie couldn't fathom him out.

Sean watched them start walking back to the hotel. He had loved someone like that not so long ago in New York. He knew Natalie wasn't what she seemed, playing him and he wondered why and how far would she go. She wasn't married to him maybe she is just a woman who likes being a mistress and likes a new man once in a while. A meet in the bar would be a good way of finding out but right now Sean had another kind of meet.

***

Craig was celebrating with Alex in the American bar of the Savoy Hotel. He had found her again the following evening sleeping round the back of the Savoy Hotel on top of the grill that produced sufficient hot air from the kitchen below. Although she smelt like a drain she still managed to look beautiful enough to take in to the bar and she even paid for the cocktails.

"We can't go on meeting like this."

"Yes, we can as long as you keep running away."

Alex looked suddenly hurt and vulnerable.

"I want to live with my dad."

"Why?" Craig genuinely had no idea why she would want to.

"Because he is the only person I can have an intelligent conversation with."

"I hadn't heard you were that clever." Craig remarked.

"Fuck you." She got up to go but Craig had no intention of losing her again.

"Come to me you can have a bath and a good night's sleep and I will sleep on the sofa."

"No Craig, we can both sleep in the bed and if I get drunk enough you can fuck me."

"Why would I want to do that?"

"Because I want you too. You keep finding me and that means you care."

185

"No, I don't. I get my orders to find you and where did you get all this money?"

"I stole it from a pimp who I didn't work for but some girls I know did and I promised to give it back to them but I'm always breaking my promises."

"OK, I think we'll go now we'll get a cab."

She had a bath hot no bubbles but she felt clean and safe and they slept in the bed and nothing happened until the next morning. They were both suddenly without warning smitten with each other and without any regret they made love.

For once he didn't care what Soames would say and he was actually looking forward to what Max might say. The phone rang and Craig was able to tell Soames she was safe and sound and that she would stay with him until she was ready to return home. He hung up on Soames and turned towards Alex soft and beautiful with no intention of going into the office and he took her in his arms again.

***

The previous evening Natalie wore a simple black dress and black shoes that quietly demonstrated how good her legs were. She smiled at Sean then at the barman and then ordered herself a double gin and tonic.

"Where's your man?"

"Working of course. Where's your lady?"

"With my future father-in-law and his royal mate."

"So, this is your stag night. Where are your male companions?"

"I don't have any."

"So, you're a loner?"

"I'd like to be but I have a mother and other obligations."

"Do you really love Maddie? Don't you think she's too young for you?"

"Of course she is but I am fond of her and our love making is sweet if not that exciting."

They talked a long time at the bar – it was a strange experience they spoke freely and found they could say anything to each other and he went willingly to her room. She decided against using the drug. It wasn't that she was afraid he might catch her out but more that she knew she could go through with it without any help and knowing Max wouldn't ask and if he did find out he would understand what happened was more natural and fully justifiable.

Whilst Sean was asleep she took the film from the camera and passed it to the contact who was waiting outside the door and from his smile she knew he had been listening. The photos would be ready to show Maddie on her wedding day.

Max opened his door and took her hand and kissed it and whispered well done in her ear.

"Go back and wake him up and come back to me once he's gone."

When she got back to her room he had gone. There was no point in worrying about what he knew or didn't know, by morning the matter would be settled.

She slept in Max's arms safe and sorry but they both knew it would never be spoken about.

The morning came too quickly and they both had a great many things to do. Max went to get the photos while Natalie went to the address where Maddie and Matthew had been staying. She took a cab and went straight upstairs to talk to Maddie and tell her what had happened the previous evening. To Natalie's' surprise Maddie smiled and simply said I expect he will stray – I'm young and inexperienced and until I get more exciting I think he will sleep with other women.

"I have photographs, Maddie."

"I would like to see them."

Natalie couldn't hide her astonishment.

Max arrived with the photographs that were supposed to bring Maddie home but Natalie stopped him going into Maddie's room.

"We are dealing with something rather bizarre, she wants to see the photos." Max turned his head sideways and his eyes registered the disbelief but he needed time to process what he had just heard.

"I'll wait downstairs."

"Max, I want you to destroy them please. They will not play a useful part in what happens today and I think you should just go back to the hotel and find the bomb."

"That's exactly what I'll do."

"All of it?"

"Yes, all of it."

"Do you have them?" Maddie was defiant.

"No, you will never see them so just prepare yourself for your wedding if you still want that."

"Will you help me get dressed and made up?"

"Of course."

"And will you come to the church with me?"

"If that's what you want."

"You are so lucky to have Max and his love I know Sean will never love me that way."

"Maddie, we could all just go home and you will find the kind of love you want."

"But I do have what I want."

"You know he's IRA."

"Yes, and I believe in his cause."

"And the violence?"

"What violence?"

Things Get Messy

As a way of forgetting what had happened the day of the wedding Natalie returned again to Hans' journal. The events of the last two days had traumatised the three of them. On the plane back to London, Maddie continued to cry and with some justification. Not only did the bridegroom die (well that's what she was told) but also her father. It didn't happen in the church or where the wedding reception was taking place but in the hotel bar. It wasn't a huge bomb, according to Max but an effective one getting both Matthew and his minor Royal friend, which according to Max were the intended targets. Sean had lured them into the bar area on the pretext of a special moment with a special whisky while he himself promptly left in order to take his mother home who had suddenly become unwell. On leaving the two elderly men, as Max observed Sean did indeed get into a car where his mother was already sat in the front passenger seat. Realising too late Max was going to the bar to warn everyone that there might be a bomb but it went off the moment he had that thought. The glass door that divided the bar from the reception had been closed by a waiter in an effort to keep the hotel guests separate from the wedding guests otherwise the death toll might have been higher.

Max looked round for Natalie who was nowhere but later appeared having been to the toilet with Maddie to help her change her hair in some way the details of which were of no interest to Max. She was safe. The bomb had killed everyone the other side of the door and the waiter who had closed it at the very moment it went off.

Natalie wasn't thinking about the events of the past two days in fact she blocked them out completely as she absorbed herself in Han's journal. She had read it many times but it was only on the plane home that she realised that a page had been torn out. It was towards the end after he had written about suicide and how he was going to do it. Why she hadn't noticed before puzzled her and as always when she wanted to know anything she turned to Max.

"There's a page missing."

"What?" Max was dosing.

"There's a page missing from his journal."

"Show me."

Max took the journal.

"No, there isn't." He gave it back to her.

"Here, look there's a small bit of paper left."

"He probably tore it out himself, he'd written something he didn't like."

Natalie accepted the explanation and Max turned away relieved.

He picked up the free newspaper provided by the airhostess and read about the bombing, 29 dead, nine were hotel staff some of whom were preparing champagne trays to bring in to the reception. Some were guests at the hotel who were in the wrong place at the wrong time and then of course the father of the bride and his friend, the minor royal. It was too early to speculate about the particular motive of this bombing. It was suggested in the article that it was just the usual IRA attempt to destabilise the North but in Max's mind there was a different motive associated with Matthew and his friend after all it was that particular hotel on that particular day.

Maddie finally stopped crying, the sleeping pill Natalie dropped into her drink had finally worked. She had already ordered a wheelchair to get her off the plane. Natalie would go straight to Matthew's house with her and stay with her while Max would drive over to their flat, which he intended to sell as soon as possible. They would move into their new home with Maddie that same evening. He looked at Natalie. Maddie's head was on her lap and she was stroking her hair. Max had to think very carefully about his next moves. Soames wouldn't be pleased at any of the outcomes and would have to accept retiring with fewer accolades than he had hoped for.

The sign came on for seat belts to be fastened, their descent had begun. Pleased to be out of Ulster but feeling quite anxious about the next few days Max hoped their new home would bring some tranquillity into their lives. He might even get a dog; the house was big enough and with the heath across the road a large hound would provide exercise and entertainment. He might also be able to have his kids staying over.

That would be a step too far – she would never allow it – she never considered Natalie stable enough but looking at her now with Maddie, Max saw Natalie's interest in the girl. He wished they could have had children.

They got a cab to the house; strangely enough Maddie had kept her keys safe and was able to open the front door. The house was chilly for a summer evening so Maddie showed Natalie how to put the central heating on.

"I'm so tired, can I go to bed please?"

"Of course, and you know we will be staying with you," Natalie said almost apologetically

"That's good, I'll need some company, and there's no one else now. Will I have to go back to school?"

"Only if you want to." Natalie had not considered the practicalities of Maddie's future life.

"I want to. I want to tell all my friends about sex with an older man."

Natalie couldn't think of anything to say.

"And I will finish my A levels. I don't think I'll be up until tomorrow." Natalie smiled. "Me neither." Natalie needed a drink and found herself laughing at Maddie's comments. She found some whisky, not a favourite drink of hers but would help pass the time until Max got back.

Max climbed the stairs towards their flat in his mind hopefully for the last time. He heard strange but recognisable sounds as he opened the front door. He almost tripped over the clothes that were piled up in front of it. A pair of flared jeans, a bra and black matching pants, a tie, a white shirt, a pair of men's underpants. As the sounds got louder Max froze. Without thinking he walked into his bedroom and saw his daughter stark naked with a man on top of her. She looked up and screeched, "Daddy!"

"Christ! Alex."

The man on top of her looked round at Max and Max who would have preferred just about anybody else's face to be looking at him saw it was Craig, slimy despicable Craig who had drugged and possibly abused Natalie and was now abusing his own daughter.

"Get off my daughter and get out." Max was frightening at this moment and didn't move, closely observing all that happened in those following moments a man post-coital and humbled. A daughter embarrassed but defiant. Max watched them both get dressed and observed how his own daughter looked him in the eye as she dressed in front of the two men, proud of her body without any hint of regret she said, "Can I go?"

"No, you stay here and explain what is going on."

Max got his gun out of his pocket and pointed it at Craig

"You ever come near my daughter again I will shoot your cock off."

Craig started to say something but thought better of it and turned to go.

Max slammed the door shut and looked at his daughter.

Natalie acquired the taste for whisky that evening as she thought about the last few days, in the course of which she almost died, had sex with another man and experienced maternal instincts she thought she didn't possess. But what obsessed her more than anything was that missing page. Max had given a plausible explanation and if indeed he was right what was it that Hans didn't want her to see? He told her everything but what if someone else hadn't wanted her to see the page or pages. But only Max knew about the journal but had never shown any inclination to read it on the grounds that he knew everything there was to know about Hans.

There was a loud knock on the front door. The clock over the fireplace stated it was 11.30 pm. She had fallen asleep in the rocking chair. The house felt too hot. When she opened the door there was Max with his 17-year-old daughter

"I found her at our flat."

"I was fucking Craig, I believe you may have fucked him too," Alex spat the words out.

"Only after he drugged me." Natalie felt she might vomit after too much whisky.

Max slapped his daughter on the face and said, "This is your last chance if, as you say you want to live with me. You never see Craig again, you treat Natalie with respect and you behave like a caring sister towards Maddie. That's the deal. Where's the whisky?"

"I may have finished it."

"You don't drink whisky."

"It tastes quite good."

"Not surprising, it's 100-year-old single malt."

"Where should I sleep, Daddy?" Alex was suddenly just his daughter again.

"There's about six bedrooms in this house I believe, so pick any one you like for tonight Max spoke with affection."

"Except where Maddie is."

"OK sure, sorry Natalie."

They all managed to smile a little.

"Christ it's hot in here" was all Max could think of saying.

"I'll go and switch the heating off. Why don't you pick a bedroom for us Max?"

The house was quiet at night and that night they all slept deeply and dreams played no part in their first night together in their new home. They all knew there was much to be done to repair whatever emotional damage had been done to them in the past few days and weeks.

Soames couldn't sleep. He knew they were back, he knew where everyone had begun the evening and where everyone had ended up. Craig had phoned him to check in, an obedient but possibly disloyal agent. Max had not communicated but that was understandable having found his daughter in bed with Craig and having a close encounter with death will have slowed him down a little. He would wait a little longer for the name of the double agent, until midday tomorrow then he would drive round to Matthew's house and wake them all up. No that's not a good idea, that would make him look desperate and Max would enjoy that too much. He might stay at home tomorrow or take Yolanda to lunch. No plenty of time for that when retirement kicked in. He would go to his office as usual and wait out the day if necessary but then he would make his move and find Max and insist on the name. The name that would bring him glory, maybe a knighthood, maybe the recognition of good services by the Queen via a letter an invite to the palace. He looked across at Yolanda. He couldn't snuggle up that evening because she had those wretched curlers in her hair. If he got too close they would stick in his eyes and make them water. At least they stopped her snoring.

Max woke early and quietly got his clothes from the floor and left the bedroom to take a shower. His first mistake on arriving in their new home was not picking the bedroom with an en-suite bathroom. He thought he would rectify that later. The question uppermost in his mind was how quickly to reveal the name of the double agent as agreed with Soames. This would be his last encounter with Soames and as such Max had to be sure he had got everything he needed from him. The thought had occurred to him that his last request might be to have Craig done away with and his daughter might have some chance of becoming a human being. He knew it was his fault as he was never there for the growing up of his first child but then how was he to know that his wife would also be a bad parent to put it mildly!

He returned to their flat to collect the post and arrange for someone to value the property. He noticed he was being followed by Soames' men, Soames must be pretty edgy. He didn't know how long he would be able to stall him and even if there was any point. He made the call to the local estate agent and to his surprise someone would come straight away to value the property and put it up for sale. He went through the post while he waited. There was bad news, his mother wouldn't last beyond the week and the letter was a week old. Not knowing didn't bother him he would just wait for the inevitable news, probably Soames would know before anybody, another reason to see him today. The other letter of interest was from the headmaster who was trying to prove the teacher was feigning a back problem. Apparently, the teacher was still at home in receipt of his salary. Max decided to pay the teacher another visit after the estate agent had been and gone.

When he opened the door, he was stunned by the beauty of the young woman standing before him. She had long very blonde natural looking hair, a smooth complexion and her blue eyes perhaps with a little too much make up stared at him unflinchingly and she smiled.

"Max, lovely to meet you, can I come in?"

"Please do." The attraction was mutual he could tell but the last thing on his mind today was sex and besides his life was complicated enough and of course there was always the strong possibility she was a plant.

He let her look around the flat on her own, he didn't offer her coffee.

"Thank you Max, I will get this all typed up for you and if you agree with our sale price we can have a board up by the end of the week."

"I'd like the board up sooner please, tomorrow if possible."

She hesitated and gave him a smile. "I'll do my best. And my name is Mandy."

He let her out and hoped he'd never have to see her again. The temptation might overcome him with all the difficulties that lay ahead he might need a diversion.

He got into his car and drove to his next destination but he didn't want anyone following him. He was lucky with the lights and losing them was easy. As he drove into the road where the teacher lived he was reminded of how quiet it was. The trees lining the street were in their full summer glory and the teacher's garden offered more places to hide. And there he was up a ladder painting the front of the house. At first Max had intended to make the teacher resign. He would force him to write the letter. But it didn't work out that way. Why this man made him so angry was difficult to say. It was as if all the tension of the last few years collided in the single moment. There was no one in the street but even so it was terribly risky. It was such a release of tension. It took all his physical strength. Why? To see if he was still capable of killing in cold blood? After all he had killed many times. He even joked to himself, if he survives the fall he would certainly have back problems. He drove away as fast as he could without looking back but keeping a careful eye on the rear-view mirror. There was no one following him. Time to go home and wake everyone up.

The house was quiet. It turned out no one was in – rather strange but it was a welcome opportunity to explore the house thoroughly, without interruption. There was what you might expect in such a large house. Downstairs there was a lounge, a study, a kitchen and a dining room. And then on the first floor there were three bedrooms two of which had en-suite bathrooms, except the one he had chosen for Natalie but he had been too tired last night to climb up to the next floor which he decided immediately would be their bedroom and the two other rooms would be a study for teach of them. Mind you there would have to be a serious redecoration programme. Matthew's taste or his dead wife's taste was hideous. The house felt like the fifties – cold drab and uninviting.

He heard the front door open and Natalie came in laughing, in fact all of them were laughing. Maddie and Alex were giggling like two teenage schoolgirls which of course was exactly who they were.

Natalie beamed at him

"We've had such a good time, we explored the area, had breakfast and bought a puppy. She is coming tomorrow and we've called her Poppy."

"Christ nothing but females in the house, why couldn't I have an Alsatian called Achilles?"

Alex went up to her father who was at the top of the stairs. She came down quickly and hugged him and whispered

"We're like your harem; who do you love the best?"

"Poppy!" He started laughing but his heart was heavy – everything comes in threes and today was such a day, possibly two deaths and one adultery considered at least.

He went towards Natalie took her hand and whispered, "Let me show you our bedroom."

It was their first time since Sean.

"Are you happy, Natalie?"

"Completely."

Their peace was interrupted by Alex who barged into the bedroom

"Christ! Alex, don't you ever knock?"

"You're not asleep so that's alright anyhow I said you were out. That guy, Craig's boss was at the door I told him I hadn't seen you as you were out."

"Did he believe you?"

"Yes, of course, Dad you know I'm a good liar."

"That's true, now get out of here and give us some peace."

"Give me some money and I'll go food shopping, Maddie and I are getting hungry."

"In my trousers on the floor over there by the window – take fifty pounds and no more."

"Can I get some wine?"

"Yes, but not the cheap stuff you have got used to."

"Bye you two – you look good together, better than you and Mum."

"Get out, Alex."

"Why are you avoiding Soames?"

"I'm just wondering if I need any more from him before I give him the name."

"Like what?"

"Come here, let's just relax in my arms and we can discuss the redecoration of this new home. I can't stand the wallpaper."

"I thought we could have a holiday while it's being done."
"It'll take a month at least so have a think."

"We'll have to take our children."

"Yes, unfortunately." And they both laughed.

Bonding

Max had never been good at parenting but Natalie turned out to be a perfect parent to two teenage girls. Firstly, the puppy was a good idea for these damaged young girls and according to Natalie their misguided emotions could now be dog-centred rather than male-centred. Max continued to remind her that the girls had exercised their own free will and had got what they deserved. Secondly, she had included them fully on the redecoration plans giving in to some of their terrible choices and thirdly she had given in to their wishes to spend a month in India. Max couldn't decide which of these three concessions made him the angriest but he relented happily in the end having been faced with three females singing from the same hymn sheet. He admitted to himself the dog was cute and as Natalie pointed out decorating needed to be done every five years by which time they would be at University or somewhere else. India did not appeal, he much preferred a beach and a boat but then something fortuitous happened. He had returned to the flat a week after they had it up for sale, just to check on the post and there was a letter addressed to The Versatile Detective Agency. I will have to change that ridiculous name he thought to himself. On opening the letter, he was quite stunned by the coincidence. It was from India, from Bombay from a man called Sabir Begum, the owner of a successful exporting business who required his assistance on a matter of 'embezzlement'. Mr Begum was coming to London for business and wanted to meet up with Max on the recommendation of his old Estonian friend Mr Soames.

The girls had taken Poppy to Hampstead Heath as they did every day since they had picked her up and as usual talked about music mainly disco divas and fashion. Alex wore jeans non-stop whereas Maddie liked maxi dresses. Alex had a short hair style

Maddie left her hair long. Alex had disliked Craig but Maddie had loved Sean. But somehow it worked.

"Show me where you slept out, please." Maddie had implored her on more than one occasion. The answer was always the same

"Dad would kill me."

"We must take Poppy home first and if Dad's busy tonight we could go to a disco first and then we can walk around my sleeping places after if you want as long as you don't tell him." They both found pleasure in the arrangement and decided to celebrate with afternoon tea in Hampstead village. The day was warm and they felt safe with each other.

Natalie was alone in the house she had come to like though not yet love. It will happen she reassured herself. There was a knock on the door and momentarily she was afraid to open it but she told herself she must. It was Soames.

"Is he in?"

"No but do come in. He's at the will reading until tonight but you are welcome to wait."

"Natalie, do you know the name?"

"Name what name?"

"Don't play games with me, young woman."

"Why would I do that? I don't know the name and I don't want to. It's between you, Max and his mother. Would you like a drink?"

"No, thank you. But tell your husband he has until tomorrow evening to give me the name. Good Day."

She was a little shaken and took herself off to bed for a nap. She took a quick look at the pages at the point where she felt something was missing from Han's journal.

She re-read the previous page.

I had never liked Max's mother. He had told me how she had been promiscuous all through his childhood, something he found painful but he shared his pain with his adopted brother Pablo. But when Pablo and his mother became lovers it was too much to bear. Neither of them understood the effect this had on Max. At that moment he must have stopped caring about everyone who was close to him past, present and future. But you saved him Natalie. I know you think he saved you but it was the other way around believe me, my sweetest Natalie. I watched and watch you with such pleasure and jealousy. But you are such an open person, I don't mean that you are naive or stupid in any way but you have an honesty combined with an ability to get at the heart of the matter. The time you asked about my parents, I could answer you honestly because you didn't want to know to hurt me you just didn't see why I should be ashamed. One of the soldiers came back. Yes, he came to say he was sorry. I was only three but my father threatened to kill him but my mother said the soldier's eyes were full of tears of remorse. He wanted her forgiveness.

We all want forgiveness. You must forgive me for what happened in Berlin. I took such a risk with your life.

Max woke her up as he got into bed; she kept meaning to have a word with him about it. It wasn't until much later she came up with the idea of a six-foot bed, one where the mattress didn't move as people got in and out of bed.

"Where are the girls? Max sounded casual but he certainly wasn't feeling casual."

"In bed, surely," Natalie replied

"No, they're not and its 12.30 am."

"Is Poppy in?"

"Yes, she's fast asleep so they haven't taken her on a walk. Natalie I'm worried."

"Well let's get up and search for them and Soames came by today. I thought you were going to give him the name anyhow he's given you until tomorrow evening."

"Natalie, I'm tired of chasing Alex around let's just stay here in each other's arms and pretend they don't exist."

"Max that's the irresponsible you that I don't love – I'm still dressed so I'll see you in the car."

Reluctantly he got dressed again, got in the car and drove into town, up and down Shaftesbury Avenue, Leicester Square, Soho, Regent Street, Waterloo and then home.

"Maybe we should have stopped and asked the vagrants?"

"They wouldn't have told us, they stick together, cover for each other in case we're police or drug dealers looking for payment."

Natalie laughed, "I don't look like a drug dealer."

"You don't look like a spy either." Max smiled.

As they drove towards the house they saw the lights on – all of them.

"I'm not looking forward to getting the electricity bill."

Natalie gave him a dirty look and said, "They're back you should be pleased."

"I am now I can go to bed."

Which is exactly what he did whereas Natalie went into the kitchen to pick a fight.

"We only went to a disco and came straight home." Alex spoke first.

"It's my fault I wanted to see London, the one Alex knows. I've lived all my life in this house, then a barn in Belfast then a farm. I know nothing about anything. I'm stupid, I fell in love with an IRA terrorist, my dad's dead and, and, and…"

The tears started flowing.

"I'm going to bed." After Alex left the kitchen Natalie took Maddie in her arms and let her cry. She couldn't think of anything constructive to say and actually wanted to go to bed herself but she now felt responsible for this girl and her future and she herself had mixed feelings about it. Had they made the right decision taking on these girls?

When she woke up the next morning Max had already gone. It was 10.30 and Natalie felt drained from the night before. The girls were still asleep and whilst making a coffee in the sparkling white kitchen she almost vomited at the foul unmistakable smell of dog shit. Her only hope was that she hadn't trod in it. Yes, there it was all over the floor by the French windows. Perhaps the dog had tried to get out.

"Poppy, Poppy, where are you?" A whimper indicated she was hiding behind the kitchen door.

"OK out you go you bad girl, into the garden." Natalie closed the door behind her and watched her run around the huge back garden which was thoroughly overgrown.

I must get a gardener she said to herself as she cleaned up the mess.

After a shower and another coffee, Natalie decided to take Poppy for a walk. Now unafraid of getting lost she ventured out with the puppy onto the heath. She kept Poppy on a lead as she was as yet untrained and would probably just run off. She had left the girls a note and wished Maddie better. Natalie lost track of time, something that she often did since Berlin. It hadn't occurred to her that the dog's howling and general bad temper was due to hunger. She wasn't hungry herself, she had lost track of time and place. She was now completely lost. She found a bench to sit on and didn't even notice when a strange man sat next to her

"Don't look at me just listen," the man said, "I will leave my newspaper and you will wait until I am out of sight and then take it with you. Don't look at the documents until you are home."

"I remember the routine," Natalie said in a shaky voice looking straight ahead.

"The way home is straight down the hill and you will get to Hampstead village. And feed the dog, he looks hungry."

Natalie was shaken at first but then anger over took her. Max promised they were out of the business.

She waited as long as she could and rushed home and hoped Max was there.

He was and she handed the newspaper

"I don't want to know anything. I'm sure it's for you anyway. I'm going to feed this damn dog and go to bed and sleep."

"Are the girls alright?"

"Yes, they're in a better state than you."

It was only 5'o clock but something told him he needed a whisky.

It was an old file, a very old file and in it there was a great deal he didn't know about his mother's activities. He settled in the comfortable armchair facing the unlit fire and slowly drank his way through the remaining whisky. Natalie came in, it must have been late, it was dark so about 10.00 pm. The long evenings were well established and created a sense of oddness. It wasn't right to have light so late.

"We both missed dinner, the girls made it but didn't want to disturb us." When Max didn't answer she said quietly, "What's the matter?"

"She's dead and this is her file, her life really." Max's face was indescribably sad, there was hurt and regret in his voice something Natalie was unaccustomed to.

"It's all here, everything. Her file is closed. They no longer have need of it."

They were both wondering the same thing. What had it all been for?

There was a knock at the door and they both knew it was Soames. Natalie walked slowly into the hallway and almost tripped over Poppy who was barking vigorously

"Good girl, Poppy," she shouted up the stairs. "Can one of you take Poppy into your room?"

"I thought she wasn't allowed upstairs?" Alex shouted back.

"Just for a couple of hours, come now please."

"OK, I'm on my way." Alex came down and Natalie let Soames in.

"I'm delighted you got this house," Natalie ignored his remark, took his jacket and placed it on the chair under the mirror by the door. She briefly looked at herself and thought she had aged.

"Will you be joining us Natalie? Only Max may wish to go over the file just with me, he might want to ask some difficult questions which you may find distressing."

"That's fine Soames just get Max to call me down. I'm going to bed to read."

"You didn't have to go to such extreme measures to get to see me Soames," Max said aggressively.

"Oh, but I did, my men have been chasing you since you got back from Belfast. I needed to get your attention. May I sit down?"

"If you must."

"May I have a drink?" Soames asked meekly.

"Aren't you driving?"

"No, not tonight." Soames took the whisky Max had poured for him.

"You can keep it, there's a lot there, too much to take in, and you'll need time. I have the original, that's just a copy well I suppose you have worked that out."

"How long were you lovers?" Max felt in the mood for directness.

"Almost four years, of course I looked very different then, not fat, some hair, well quite a bit actually."

"Did she love you?"

"I think so, well actually yes, she said she did."

"Why did it stop?"

"Because she crossed to the other side like Pablo, well you were there in Florida, you worked it out."

"So, you knew but you pretended you didn't in order to feed them false information."

"Max that's how it works, you know that."

"Did Pablo usurp your place? Is that why you played with him all those years he was in Berlin?"

"Max, believe it or not I'm not a jealous man. I had no right to be, I was married. It didn't matter how many lovers she had or who they were but she was an extraordinary woman and she loved you greatly."

There was a long pause. Max refilled their glasses and he finally sat down in the chair opposite Soames. They both sipped their drinks silently.

"I won't be able to tell her who it is and you must swear you will keep it from her."

"Of course I won't tell her. That explains the mess in Berlin."

"How did we miss it, Soames?"

"Easy, he was a clever but rather damaged human being, his background you know."

"Oh, come on Soames there must have been suspicions."

"I suspect everyone, as you are well aware but Hans was always considered sound by my superiors. He had every good reason to hate the Russians."

"So, who or what turned him?" Max had almost forgotten he was speaking to his former boss whom he detested.

"His father I suppose."

"Not his German father surely?"

"No, no, not at all. The Russian soldier that came to see him after you recruited him who claimed to be his real father."

"What, what are you talking about?"

"They formed a relationship, they bonded you know his real father comes back, takes him fishing, all that nonsense."

"It's in his journal well in the pages that are torn out. Well not the same ones you tore out. You see he wanted her to know and he gave her the reasons why but we got to it before she did and I must say we made a better job of disguising it than you did."

"Well I was in a hurry. I expect you had all the time you needed." Max was furious with himself for thinking he had any hold over Soames. He already knew Hans was the double agent.

"So why did you help us in Belfast?"

"Intelligence gathering that's all. Just another opportunity without getting the service directly involved."

"Won't this spoil your retirement glory?"

"I don't think so Max. I've something else up my sleeve you'll see. Now, I think your wife is waiting for you in bed as is mine."

Max felt quite nauseous at the implication of this remark. The thought of Soames still having a sex life filled him with horror. He had a lot to take in, especially Soames and his mother. His mind was spinning not with the whisky but the salacious details of his mother's life. Was this all that she was, a sex-driven double agent with her loyalties shifting according to her lovers? There must be more to this woman.

Natalie was asleep or at least pretended to be and Max couldn't have been more relieved.

Whatever she did or didn't know had not seemed to cause any negative change in her. In fact, she seemed rather contented, energised and he wished he felt the same. He felt anxious, no doubt brought on by confronting his past by reading his mother's file.

He had performed a violent act on a man who didn't deserve it and he had entered into an adulterous relationship with the woman who was selling their flat. He felt ashamed and wished he were another person free from it.

There was a way out and tomorrow he would accept the assignment in India. Before that he would burn his mother's file as an act of defiance against her and the service. He had told Mandy it was over. She wasn't too pleased; in fact, she made a terrible scene. He had foolishly taken her out to dinner by way of preparing her – a very stupid idea. He would have to make his agency work for him and Natalie and the other two females in his life that somehow, he couldn't turn his back on. So much would have to remain unsaid. He wondered if he should tell her about the page he had torn out so clumsily but why disturb her equilibrium.

Un-Bonding

When he heard the door, he thought Soames had returned for the file and he was reluctant to relinquish it. Besides he thought to himself there was no point in taking it back, he had his own copy. Or he may have left something innocuous like a scarf or a pair of gloves. Max looked round the room, just empty glasses and an almost empty bottle of whisky. The knock came again even louder, he would have to answer it. The blond woman stood boldly on the doorstep. He could barely remember her name. He froze and she smiled.

"It's all right you don't have to let me in. I just wanted to see where you live."

"Go away, didn't you get my correspondence?"

"Is she upstairs, your Natalie. Does she know? I can see by your expression she doesn't have a clue, does she? Shall I shout out to her, shall I?"

"What do you want?"

"One more fuck that's all and I'll disappear." Max was furious and went to shut the door. He wasn't sure whether this was a clever or very stupid move. Her foot was in the door.

"Ouch baby. Come tomorrow to the flat tomorrow or she will know by the end of the day."

"Okay." Max again tried to shut the door.

"I'll expect you at ten in the morning, goodnight."

He managed to get the door shut before virtually collapsing behind it. He sensed she was still there and when the letterbox opened and she blew him a kiss he wanted to kill her.

"What are you doing, Dad?" He got himself up from the floor. He was dizzy with all the drink and talk about his mother. She looked beautiful with her short dark hair, his colour exactly but straight not wavy. She had put on his dressing gown; it was too long for her. She sat at the top of the stairs hugging her knees.

"Just saying goodnight to Soames. Let me lock up now honey." As he performed the essential nightly procedure, the chain, the bolt, the chubb he sensed she was still there. His daughter hadn't moved either. He managed to say, "Is Maddie asleep?"

"Yes, she always goes to sleep first."

"In her own room yet?" Max hovered round the front door.

"No, she's still in mine."

"I'll have to order a double bed for you."

"OK, that would be good, goodnight."

Max thought about the remark later, he looked through the peephole, she had gone. He listened; he heard the car drive away. He broke out into a sweat as he climbed the stairs. The deep maroon carpet swirled around in front of him. He hated it, it had to go.

Soames' words came back to him.

"Are you really happy Max? India? Embezzlement? Not really your sort of thing. I'm almost sorry I told my old school friend about you."

"Anything to get away from you Soames."

"Are you sure it's me you're running from. I'll be gone soon enough. You might even miss me. In any case Max I'll always be on your side, so do call me if you need my help."

He knows, he fucking knows. He recalled Soames' face as he said, "Are you sure it's me you're running from?" For such an obese man, Soames' face was always expressive from the raising of the eyebrows to the way he would tilt his head to the left side always the left side, the sniff when he told a lie. The I-told-you-so way he pushed his lips together and looked like he was blowing you a kiss. The tone of voice was trickier, it was expressionless the purpose of which was to make the listener believe in what he was saying; it became a fact. As he slid in slowly and silently next to Natalie he had no idea what to do. The last thing he wanted to do was to return to the flat the next day but what to do about her. He lay awake most of the night apart from making a phone call and as he returned to bed Natalie woke up and wanted to make love. He had never refused her before.

"Sorry darling, I've got a few loose ends to tie up and it a matter of some urgency."

"I can wait till later." And she turned over and went back to sleep. Max showered, the water was cold because someone had forgot to put it on but it had the right effect, it energised him making him positive, well that's what he told himself. He went down to the kitchen. He didn't like Matthew's taste, crass cupboard colour, yellow for Christ's sake, no good with a hangover. Nothing worked properly, everything needed replacing, he would get that organised while they were away, if they ever went. He stubbed his toe as he sat down waiting for the coffee machine to do its thing but the coffee smell couldn't hide the distinctive smell of dog shit. "Where are you, fucking dog?"

Poppy was hiding having realised even at such a young age she had done something wrong. He retched when he saw it just where he had sat, under the table. He rushed to the downstairs bathroom (thank god for that) he thought to himself as he puked into the toilet. He felt better and as he grabbed the puppy by the scruff of its neck and threw it into the garden. Soames' words came back to him…

"Trust you to fuck a psychopath."

The dog was not very intelligent he decided because instead of staying out of sight in the garden she was looking pleadingly at him from the other side of the glass door as if he would let her back in. He left the mess and went looking for a pair of shoes, none under the stairs, the dog was now whining and whinging, he realised he hadn't locked that back door from the night before so he found the keys in a jar on the window sill in full view. He enjoyed locking the dog out. *She's probably hungry but I won't be feeding her,* he said to himself. "Stay there you bitch." He returned to the bedroom and scuffled around the wardrobe and heard Natalie murmuring but he tried to make a hasty exit.

"The girls are getting on well, aren't they?"

"Rather too well if you ask me."

"What do you mean?"

"Lesbians." He surprised himself when he came straight out with it.

"Good for them if it's true."

"What happens when they break up?" Max retorted.

"Good point. I think I'll come to the flat today – the Americans call it closure. I'll have a quick shower."

"I was going out for breakfast," Max said without thinking.

"Good, I'll join you."

The phone rang and with great relief and Soames was the caller.

"Natalie's coming to the flat." Max was out of breath ensuring he and only he answered the phone.

"And you don't want the estate agent to be there."

"Precisely."

"Get there by 11 am at the earliest."

"What time is it now?" Max asked genuinely having lost all sense of time.

"Only 8.15. You've plenty of time for breakfast."

"You look like you've seen a ghost."

Max watched her get dressed, the phone rang again but this time he knew it was her. He shuddered to think of it all, the risk he was taking, the risk he had taken. She didn't speak perhaps realising Natalie was there with him but that wouldn't matter to her. He hung up.

"Let's go to Café Mozart," Natalie's voice brought him back

"I don't know if they do breakfast."

"Well let's go and see."

"The dog crapped again in the kitchen, I think we should let the girls clear it up, don't you?"

"Absolutely." Natalie was now fully dressed and made it clear she was ready to go.

They walked hand in hand along the pavement by the Heath. It was a beautiful August morning warm with the promise of a warm day but always with a hint of cloud and rain. Natalie noticed his hands were sweaty and she removed hers. He didn't seem to notice.

When they arrived it was just opening. "Can you order for me? I need the toilet." The waiter heard him and pointed him in the right direction. He was in luck there was a public phone.

He called the flat, a strange voice answered, "Not yet mate give us another hour at least, longer if you can." Max didn't have a chance to get any further news as the man put the phone down.

"Natalie, I'm just popping back to get the car. We'll need it to go to the flat."

"Have your breakfast first Max."

"Lost my appetite, you eat it for me."

Both Natalie and the waiter had the same expression of bewilderment on their faces.

He jogged back feeling sick to the stomach at what he thought he had colluded with.

It was all so drastic; everything in his life was always so dramatic. His wife, his ex-wife, his children. He felt too old for it all. India was his way out. Yes, he wanted to get away from it all. He could hear the dog barking in the garden so he allowed it through the front door. Thank god there weren't neighbours to worry about. The house was about as well detached as it could be in London. He got the car keys from the bowl on the shelf in the hallway. It was about the only thing familiar to him. The girls were still in bed and apart from an overexcited puppy panting away the house was pretty silent. He was tempted to look in on them but that was paranoia, of course they were fine asleep in each other's arms.

He arrived back and the waiter presented him with scrambled eggs on brown toast.

"Are they meant to be sloppy and what's the green stuff?"

"Chives, I got him to hold off making them till you got back."

"Makes a change from sausages and bacon but don't think I'm becoming a vegetarian in India."

"Well the girls have been researching and apparently it's best with our English tummies."

"Nothing wrong with my tummy and they're not even up yet."

"Well it's still early and they've had a tough time."

"Both of their own choosing."

"What's the matter with you today, Max, you're so grumpy?"

"Let's pay the man and go for a drive. The estate agent isn't ready for us to sign off yet."

Max needed the toilet, must be nerves, I'm too young for prostate trouble he thought to himself. Just as he got down the stairs, the phone rang. Picking it up seemed the most natural thing to do.

"When you're ready" was all he said. The same man's voice. I'll piss in the flat I can wait he said out loud and rushed up the stairs. Natalie was waiting by the car.

"Were going straight there."

"But I thought you said they weren't ready."

"Did I?"

As they drove down into their road it seemed quiet enough. Funny Max thought he had never noticed it was tree lined, the

210

leaves made quite a difference. As they got out of the car, there was a cool breeze. It was about 9.00 am he supposed but he wasn't supposed to meet her until 10.00 am. As he parked up outside the apartment block he wondered if this was some kind of a trap. Was Mandy going to be there? Was she going to confront him and Natalie? How would she know Natalie was here?

"Why don't you wait in the car Natalie?"

"Because I want closure." There was irony in her words.

"Just let me go up first, will you?"

"Whatever's bothering you, Max, we share it, OK?"

He didn't answer as she followed him up the stairs. He never enjoyed reaching this door. He had opened the door to the sounds of his own daughter fucking a creep. And on the first occasion he was innocently collecting the post she opened the door stark naked. She was holding the post between her legs. He saw her twice after that and made it clear the third time it would be the last. The door was ajar and behind it was that cheerful cockney voice, "Hello, we were able to clear everything up much earlier than expected." The flat was empty and spotless.

"All the stuff is being stored for you as agreed with you, sir."

Max rushed past him to the bathroom.

The man smiled at Natalie who smiled back. Max emerged looking better.

"Who bought it?" Natalie thought that was a reasonable question to ask though both men looked surprised by the question.

"I can have the details sent over if you require them."

"No, we don't, thanks," Max said as he handed over the keys.

"Well now if you could just put your signature on this for me, sir."

"Don't I need to sign?" Again, both men seemed to react strangely to this request.

"Well if you wish, madam."

"Let's go, Natalie." And he grabbed her arm rather roughly she thought.

As they got in the car she asked, "Did you notice the stain in the hallway?"

"Err, yes that was me I spilt some coffee when I bent down to collect the post one day."

"On the way in or on the way out?"

"Sorry." Max looked quizzically

"Never mind. Who did we sell it to?"

"Some woman, I don't remember her name."

Natalie lost interest and said, "Let's take the girls out to lunch and celebrate."

Max didn't answer straightaway. He had only just emptied the breakfast unable to keep it down.

"Can we do dinner instead? Not really ready for lunch."

"OK that would be just as good, even better."

Max didn't drive straight home. She knew not to ask any more questions.

They arrived home at midday, fed the dog, cleaned up the mess which was now dried and surprisingly odourless. Max went upstairs and said with authority, "I'm going for a nap, don't let anyone disturb me."

"I won't," Natalie said with assurance. First Max rang Soames.

"You didn't say Natalie would be with you."

"Sorry, she insisted."

"Well it certainly created a stir, actually it helped, they worked more quickly."

"And thoroughly I hope, she noticed the stain in the hall way."

"Good girl, I told you she'd make a good spy eventually."

"Actually, Soames you said quite the opposite."

"Did I?"

"So, who bought the flat?"

"We did."

"You and Yolanda?"

"No, us, the service. We needed a safe house in that area so we've taken it off your hands."

"But we need the money, Soames."

"Rest assured you have it, in fact go to the bank it's in your account already. We've paid off the mortgage and given you a bit of a bonus."

"What about her?"

"Do you really want to know the details?"

Max was silent.

"When are you off to India?"

"I haven't arranged that yet. Probably October, maybe earlier."

"I have a contact there if you need my help to settle in."

"We're only going for a month."

"Let's hope so I want you back for my retirement do at Christmas."

Max said goodbye, got into the unmade bed and slept at last.

It wasn't until the plane took off at Heathrow that Max saw the headline in the complimentary newspaper.

Young female Estate Agent Goes Missing. Police stepping up their investigation.

He started to read it. Apparently, the police had revealed her work diary stated how she had an appointment with a Mr. M on the morning her mother said she disappeared.

He looked at Natalie sitting beside him and so badly wanted to tell her. Across the aisle were the two young women who had come to live with them. They were holding hands.